"You may not be quite devastatingly beautiful, but you are most desirable, you know."

She was not entirely oblivious of his intention. But she was too astonished by it to put up any defense—even if she'd wished to do so. His kiss belonged to an entirely different category than the few chaste busses she'd previously experienced. It was almost as pleasurable as it was disturbing.

"Damnation!"

"Well, thank you very much. I know I'm hardly as experienced as you seem to be, but I'd expect a better review than that for my performance."

His laugh was genuine. "Eliza, in our brief acquaintance the only thing I can be sure of about you is that you will never react like any other female."

Also by Marian Devon
Published by Fawcett Books:

ESCAPADE
FORTUNES OF THE HEART
GEORGIANA
THE HEATHER AND THE BLADE
A QUESTION OF CLASS
SIR SHAM

Miss Osborne Misbehaves

Marian Devon

FAWCETT CREST · NEW YORK

Chapter
One

"*Traveling alone then, are we, miss?*"
Miss Eliza Osborne had been sizing up her
fellow passengers with something bordering on
alarm. The dozen or so people stood, more scattered
than grouped, in the courtyard of the Blossoms Inn
watching four skittish horses being harnessed to a
stagecoach that would take some of them all the
way to Brighton. Unconsciously she'd inched nearer
to the most respectable-looking member of the mot-
ley group. He had asked the question.

"Well, no, not alone precisely. That is to say, I
traveled up to London with friends. And"—she
somehow felt the need to add a whisker—"I'm being met, of course."

"I see."

The kindly stranger appeared to see at that, for
he gave her a knowing look that had "runaway"
written all over it. He was a small man, well

dressed, and seemed every inch the gentleman. His cockney voice, however, had destroyed that impression. Still, the fatherly smile he gave Eliza was most reassuring.

"Well, you want to watch out for yourself, miss. Can't be too careful. There's them as sees a pretty young female traveling alone that'll try to take advantage by getting overfamiliar-like. Especially seeing as 'ow she's the only female passenger in the lot."

Miss Osborne had already taken note of that lowering circumstance. She had counted on some respectable farmer's wife to whom she could attach herself, but none of that comfortable species was to be seen among the disreputable-looking males eyeing the horses.

"I don't want to put you into a taking or anything like that." The fatherly man, who'd been speaking low, now further reduced his volume to a whisper. "But the fact of the matter is—and I couldn't say fairer to me own daughter—that you get all kinds of riffraff riding the public coaches these days." He ran an assessing eye over her gray bombazine traveling costume, which was proving warm in the summer midday and did little to set off her dark brown hair and eyes. Despite these drawbacks, it still managed to advertise her class. "Types that a lady like yourself ain't in the habit of rubbing elbows with, I'll wager. Now you take that cove standing over there, for instance. You probably didn't 'appen to notice it, but for some time now 'e's been staring your way."

Eliza had noticed, all right. Indeed it had been that same intense blue-eyed gaze that had sent her sidling closer to the fatherly person, trying to give the impression that they were traveling together.

There was something altogether too disturbing about the young man's appearance. For one thing, he didn't seem to have ever heard of soap and water: he was filthy from head to toe. A stubble of blond beard further marred a face that might have been considered handsome if it hadn't brought to mind visions of certain buccaneers of the more unpleasant sort. (A prominent scar on his right cheekbone possibly helped to account for this cutthroat image.) The fact that his filthy clothes, from a battered curly-brimmed beaver down to a grimy, scuffed-up pair of Hessian boots that had long since forfeited up their tassels, still smacked of Bond Street was somehow appalling. Such decadence spoke of opium dens or other horrors beyond the scope of the sheltered Miss Osborne's imagination.

"You wouldn't think to see 'im now," Eliza's confidant continued, "but that man yonder is one of the nobs. A gentleman 'e was. But a word of warning to ye, miss. When you board the stagecoach, steer as clear of 'im as possible. Straight out of Newgate 'e is, and that's a fact."

"Newgate!" Miss Osborne's voice cracked in horror. London's infamous prison was well known, even in the provinces. Her exclamation must have had carrying power, for the gaolbird's gaze, which had momentarily shifted to the harnessing, flickered their way again.

"Sssh!" The fatherly man shook his head in caution. "Didn't wish to call 'is attention back to you. Just felt the need to warn ye, miss, that's all." He suddenly began to back away as the tall ex–Newgate resident started to move toward them.

"Where are you going?" Eliza whispered in alarm. "Please don't leave me. I'd like to sit by you in the coach."

"Oh, I'm not taking the coach, miss," the little man said hurriedly. "Just like to see it orf, that's all. Due at me office now. 'Ave a good trip!" He wheeled abruptly, then broke into a run.

Miss Osborne screamed as the ex-convict sprinted toward her. But he passed her by without a glance,

3

in hot pursuit of the little man who was headed for the courtyard gate at an amazing speed that still failed to outstrip the long legs racing behind him. Eliza's acquaintance was brought down with a flying tackle while she ran, screeching, to his aid. "Help! Murder!" was the tenor of her cries.

There was a brief struggle in the dust, but claw, kick, writhe, and curse though he might, the little man was no match for the taller, younger one on top. Just as a crowd collected to cheer the combatants on, the former Newgate resident released his victim and rose to his feet, clutching a reticule.

"I think this belongs to you." While holding aloft a small gray bag, he turned an ironic gaze on Miss Osborne. The sight of her purse effectively cut off her screeches. The little man picked himself up out of the dirt and bolted.

"My reticule!" Eliza gasped. "He stole my reticule!" The crowd, robbed of further excitement, melted away. "And you let him get away," she added indignantly.

The gaolbird shrugged. "I retrieved your purse, which is far more to the point."

"There's also the principle of justice—" she began with righteous indignation, only to break off in confusion as it occurred to her that he might not be a receptive target for such moralizing.

He picked up on her embarrassment with a smile that proved no more than a baring of straight white teeth. "You're right, of course. I've no high opinion of justice. It is my opinion, though, that a flat like you should be content to get your purse back and to have learned a valuable lesson."

Though Eliza wasn't precisely sure just what a flat was, she colored all the same. "Well, he certainly seemed like a perfectly respectable— Oh, I say! Just what do you think you're doing, sir?"

The question was rhetorical. It was more than

obvious that the disreputable young man was rifling through her reticule.

"Collecting my reward," he replied as he totted up the currency he'd found there. "Oh, good. I see you can afford to pay my fare and still have a bit left over." He coolly pocketed some of her money, then handed her the bag.

"Well, it was certainly considerate of that other man to snatch this and save you the bother," she remarked bitterly as she began to tie together the purse strings that the fatherly man had cut.

"Oh, come now." There was genuine amusement in the ex-convict's tone. "Where's your celebrated sense of justice got to? Surely I deserve something for my pains. And you have your reticule back. With all the rubbish that's crammed in it, it must have some value for you. Besides, I intend to pay you back, though I hardly expect you to believe that."

Miss Osborne's sniff was eloquent.

"Come on," he said. "We'd best get aboard." She followed his gaze to the coach, where the coachman was climbing onto his perch. "I've no desire to sit on top. It looks like rain."

But once they were inside and she was jammed between him and a fat countryman with an equally fat brown-paper parcel on his bulging knees, she could only wish that either her companion or herself had opted for a seat in the open air. Whereas the sweaty parcel-holder was not exactly a bouquet of flowers, the aroma that arose from the Newgate bird was almost unbearable.

As the coachman sprang his horses and they clattered through the arched inn-yard gate and onto the thoroughfare, Eliza concentrated upon not lurching against her fellow passengers while she fished into her recovered reticule for a handkerchief. She tried to be unobtrusive about this operation, but he raised a single eyebrow as she pulled out the wisp of linen and held it to her nose.

"Want to sit by the window?" he asked politely. "I'd forgotten how rank I must be. You become rather inured to odor in my former residence."

"Thank you," she murmured as he lowered a window. Then she climbed across his knees.

Though the air of London left a lot to be desired, it was still preferable to the aroma within the coach. She gulped in grateful lungsful while beside her the criminal eased himself down in the seat and stretched out his long legs, to the detriment of two pairs of boots opposite that had to rearrange themselves to make room for his. He closed his eyes and was soon asleep.

As the coach clattered its way through the bustle and the clamor that was London, Miss Eliza Osborne could not take in the exotic sights for thinking of all the things Papa would say (if he were not, that is, first felled by a sudden stroke of apoplexy) if he could see her now, riding in a public coach in the company of an ex-convict straight from Newgate.

She turned then and stole a wary glance at her sleeping companion. Admittedly, he looked less sinister in this unguarded moment with his knowing eyes now shuttered, his face wiped clean of expression, if not of grime, and his lips slightly parted as he breathed slowly in and out.

Uneasily, she began to wonder just what crime or crimes he might be guilty of. He'd been a gentleman, of that she'd little doubt. There was the questionable word of the purse snatcher, of course. And the clothes that had once seen much better days. But more than that, unlike her cutpurse friend, this man was quite well spoken, with an accent that left little question as to his class.

The most likely possibility, she collected, was that he'd been incarcerated for unpaid debts. This had been the gentleman's crime for donkey's years. And now in 1816 gambling was still all the rage, and living beyond one's means had become the accepted mode for young members of the ton.

But even so she somehow doubted that the man beside her had been imprisoned for anything quite so tame. Perhaps it was the livid scar that made her think so. Or the pantherlike leap that had brought the cutpurse down. But for whatever reason, Eliza sensed that there was something violent in his makeup that suggested crimes of a more passionate nature than unpaid debts. The possibility that she could be seated next to a murderer insinuated itself into her thinking until the idea became fixed.

Then, with a supreme effort of will, she managed to thrust the ex-convict from her mind and turned her attention to the window once again. They were leaving the city behind now, and she gratefully breathed in the fresh country air. Up above them the coachman's yard of tin blasted forth a warning as they approached a curve. The horses took it at full gallop and the coach swung wide. Eliza grabbed the strap to steady herself as the other passengers shifted on the seats. But when the head of the sleeping murderer came to rest upon her shoulder and remained there, it took all her mustered willpower to repress a shriek.

Chapter Two

S ince this was Eliza's first experience of a public coach, she'd no comparison for the driver's skill in handling his equipage. But they did seem to be weaving unnecessarily, as if their coachman was overcontrolling his galloping cattle. She wondered also at his speed. Though she welcomed progress on such a hideous journey, she feared that at this rate the horses would soon be exhausted.

A sudden swerve sent the blond head in the disreputable beaver rolling off her shoulder. The gentleman sat up. "I think our coachman's foxed," he observed. "I noticed he'd fortified himself back at the Blossoms, but he must have brought along a bottle as well. His driving's going from bad to worse."

"You haven't been asleep!" she accused indignantly.

"Well, no." He grinned. "It's just that where I've

been there weren't any . . . pillows. I couldn't resist the temptation to take advantage."

The weasely man opposite, who appeared to have been trying to size up this strange twosome ever since they'd boarded and whose wandering legs Eliza had kept avoiding, now inquired, "You two together, are you?"

Eliza opened her mouth to deny this hotly, but the man next to her interposed pleasantly. "Why, yes. My sister came up to London for my come-out."

"Your come-out?"

"Newgate. Released this morning."

This announcement considerably increased their space in the crowded coach as the others shrank away.

"I'd give my kingdom for a cigar right now," the gaolbird murmured.

If any of the passengers possessed the means to blow a cloud, no offer was forthcoming. Thank goodness, Eliza thought. She was beginning to feel decidedly queasy. Cigar smoke would be the outside of enough.

Now that her companion had shocked the other passengers into silence, he seemed to feel an obligation to fill the void. "Storm coming," he remarked as he peered past Eliza at the rapidly darkening sky. "Let's hope our inebriated friend up there can hold his team."

The hope soon died. For as the coach and a thunderstorm approached each other, the passengers were dashed wildly from side to side. The man beside Eliza threw an arm around her, whether to anchor himself or her she'd no idea. In any case, she gave him a speaking look to let him know just what she thought of his overfamiliarity. He shrugged and then withdrew it at the very moment when a wheel struck an obstacle in the road and she was jolted to the floor. There was a decided I-told-you-so look in the vivid blue eyes as he dragged

9

her back into place. This time she hadn't the face to object to the strong arm around her shoulders.

The heavens opened and the deluge hit. The gallows-bird released his hold and struggled to close the window before they drowned. He had just settled back and replaced his arm, while bracing his battered boots on the opposite seat between two bouncing passengers, when a vertical bolt of lightning made contact with a nearby tree, resulting in a flash and a crack that spurred the exhausted horses into a new burst of panicked speed.

"O-oh m-my g-goodness!" Eliza exclaimed through rattling teeth in order to head off a scream. The other passengers were also giving tongue. Their comments would have put her to the blush had she not been far too frightened to take notice. Cries of terror from the drenched outside passengers added to her fright. And when the wheels' sudden collision with a boulder sent them bouncing around inside like India-rubber balls, she knew it must be the end and perceived the storm as divine retribution for her folly.

The coach wobbled wildly on its way for a few more seconds. Then her companion warned, "Hang on! The wheel's going!" just before there was a sickening lurch and a bone-rattling thud, and the six passengers were sent tumbling toward the right front corner where once a wheel had been.

Even as she was thrown, Eliza was aware of two circumstances: one, passengers were jumping or being jolted from the coach roof, and two, her own position guaranteed that she would land atop the inside heap.

There were cries and curses all around. "Get orf me!" from the bottom of the interior pile of bodies seemed to be the most insistent. It penetrated Eliza's terror and made her conscious of a duty to comply since she was at the pinnacle of their mound. She forced herself to release the handfuls of filthy coat she'd been clutching and inch her way, crablike, back up the inclined coach.

"Are you all right?" asked the gaolbird from behind her, as, on hands and knees, he reached around to force the coach door open. In their position this was like opening the deck hatch of a ship's hold. He pulled himself out first, then reached in to haul her and the others up and out.

"Well, at any rate the storm's over," the criminal remarked with an attempt at cheerfulness. And even in her battered, benumbed state Eliza could not help thinking, What a pity. He'd certainly have been none the worse for a good drenching.

By some miracle none of the passengers was seriously hurt, though there'd be lumps and bruises to contend with and one man had twisted his ankle when he jumped down off the roof. This unfortunate occupied his time by removing his boot and wrapping his neckerchief tightly around the swelling, while his fellow passengers angrily converged upon the coachman.

It was that worthy's opinion that he couldn't be held responsible for an act of God. It was the consensus of his passengers that if he hadn't been shooting the cat all day, he could have controlled his cattle.

The ex-Newgate man and Miss Osborne stood on the fringe of the uproar. "Come on," he said abruptly. "The good news is we're not over three or four miles away from East Grinstead. We're supposed to change horses at the White Hart there."

Eliza's reluctance to set off down the tree-lined road in tandem must have shown, for he frowned impatiently. "Point one, you're safe as houses with me. And two, if you feel more comfortable with that rabble"—he jerked a thumb toward the angry huddle around the protesting coachman—"it's just one more evidence of your faulty judgment."

"What do you mean 'one more evidence'?" she

retorted as she fell into step beside him. "What could you possibly know about my judgment?"

"Enough. I saw you gulled by Gentleman Jack Oliver, remember."

"Gentleman Jack? Oh." Her face went pink. "The man who stole my purse, you mean."

"Exactly." They were walking down the road at a rapid clip. The other members of their party had begun to follow, several yards behind. "When you first got worried, back at the posting house, about the questionable company you were keeping, you unerringly picked out the biggest scoundrel in the lot to turn to for protection."

"The *biggest* scoundrel?" Her tone was rife with meaning as she lengthened her stride to keep up with him.

"Yes." The blue eyes dared her to contradict him.

She took the dare. "Well, he didn't speak too highly of you, either."

"Naturally. He had to pin your attention on something in order to lift your purse. I was a natural target."

"Well, you had been staring at me," she said defensively.

"I hate to prick your vanity, but I was more interested in watching Gentleman Jack Oliver operate. I knew he'd picked you for his mark and I was curious to see just how he'd go about relieving you of your reticule."

"Oh, I see. He also took me for a flat, then."

"Did I call you that? Well, since a flat's someone who's easily gulled, the term obviously fits. But I should not have used it. Most rag-mannered of me. Blame the company I've been keeping recently. And the fact that I don't know your proper name." He paused expectantly.

"Miss Osborne," she muttered.

"And I'm Mr. Slaughter." He mimicked her grudging tone. "And do you mind saying just why the obviously respectable Miss Osborne is traveling so unrespectably to Brighton?"

Since she'd just bent over to remove a pebble from her slipper, Eliza's reply was muffled. "I'm not going to Brighton. I'm going to visit my aunt in Claxton." She straightened. "And I didn't see anything so scandalous about a day trip on a public coach. Though now"—her face reflected her distress—"heaven knows when we'll ever get there."

"Claxton? That's where I'm going. Who is your aunt? In a place that small there can't be many possibilities."

It struck her then that divine retribution for her impulsive decision to strike out on her own was working overtime. First the bolt of lightning. Now the revelation that she and this disreputable stranger had one and the same destination. "My aunt is Mrs. Tomkins," she replied.

"The vicar's wife? Well, I did say you were respectable, did I not? But, more important, that would make you a, uh, relation of Lord Wenham."

"It would not." She was hot, tired, and irritable, and nettled by his tone. "My aunt's husband is a *poor* relation of Lord Wenham. That was what you were going to say, wasn't it? But I'm no kin of his."

"Oh, well. No matter. The vicar's relationship will gain you easy access to the Hall. You'll have no trouble meeting the Honorable Jervis at all."

"And just who exactly is the Honorable Jervis? And just why might I wish to meet him?" she haughtily inquired.

"Oh, come now." He looked amused. "The lady doth protest too much. The good vicar's niece—in-law, that is—and arriving just before the coming-of-age celebration. You won't bam me into believing that you never heard of Jervis Wenham. They tell me that the number of females being flung at his head just now is remarkable, indeed. But I'll wager you're the first to arrive by public coach."

The look she gave him was withering, but her tone was sugar-sweet. "Are you sure you weren't just released from Bedlam and not Newgate? Now listen closely while I repeat: I haven't the slightest notion who the Honorable Whoever is—nor have I any desire to know."

"Not even for a fortune and the prospect of a title?" His lip curled cynically. "Miss Osborne, you astound me. Still, perhaps you're telling the truth. Very well, then, you *are* telling the truth," he amended as she bristled. "Which is just as well. For it's only fair to warn you that if you should have any intention of setting your cap for the Honorable Jervis Wenham, forget it. You're a very attractive young lady, Miss Osborne, but I'm afraid you'd find yourself quite overmatched. Oh, no need to take offense. The same could be said of all the other contenders for that matrimonial prize. The blunt truth is, no female alive is any match for the diamond of the first water who's just entered the lists."

The ex-convict's mood had swiftly changed. His voice had become so bitter and his scowl so fierce that Eliza instinctively inched away from him as they trudged up a hill.

Chapter Three

The White Hart was a welcome sight. Eliza's soft
kid slippers had not been intended for heavy
walking and her feet were becoming sore. She
limped after Mr. Slaughter, who headed directly for
the courtyard pump where a team was being wa-
tered at the trough. Eliza toyed with the idea of
sitting on the ground while the cattle took their
dainty time, looking up frequently to whinny and
to send drops spraying off their muzzles. She resisted this notion, however. Any more contact with
nature's dirt and the filth left behind by humans
and animals and she'd soon be looking as scruffy as
her companion.

"Would you mind pumping?" he inquired politely as the last horse backed away. Though she
privately thought, Ladies first, and wondered why
they didn't get their drinks of water, properly contained within glasses, inside the inn, she nodded.

Then, as she grasped the iron handle and began to ply it up and down . . . "What on earth do you think you're doing?" she gasped. He'd removed his coat and waistcoat and was now working on the buttons of an unspeakable shirt, which was reduced almost to rags.

"I'm about to wash. And don't tell me you haven't been longing for me to do it ever since we met. Pump away!"

She resumed her operation. As the water gushed over his head and bare shoulders, he splashed and rubbed his hair, face, arms, and chest vigorously. She momentarily closed her eyes in accordance with the sudden conviction that this had to be a dream. There was no way in actuality that she, Miss Eliza Osborne, the respectable daughter of Sir Charles Osborne, could actually be assisting a murderer to bathe.

"You can stop now."

She opened them, and it was no dream. The ex-convict stood before her, from the waist upward as bare as when he was born. She was hit by a confusion of impressions: broad shoulders, dark chest hair in contrast to the fair locks on his head, muscular but thin. She could count his ribs if she were so inclined.

"Well, that's the best I can do without benefit of soap," he was saying as he picked up his filthy shirt and eyed it dubiously. "Do you suppose— I say, what's the matter?" She had given a sudden gasp.

Her furtive, embarrassed assessment of his physique had just now focused on a scar—long, jagged, wicked, and recent—in the area near his heart.

"Oh, yes, that." He followed her gaze and gave a rueful shrug. "A fellow lodger tried to hone his carving technique. Looks worse than it was, actually. No need to turn so green.

"As I was about to say, and I hate to ask it, do you think you could lend me the price of a clean

16

shirt? If memory serves me right, you still have a few pounds left in your reticule."

She was still staring at his chest. The slash resembled a bolt of streaked lightning.

"I don't like to keep pointing this out," he continued when she failed to reply, "but if I hadn't tackled old Gentleman Jack back there at the Blossoms, your own financial situation would be as bad as mine. Besides, we are speaking of a loan, merely. Miss Osborne!"

"What?" She snapped back to reality from her nightmare of the dark world of prison violence. "I'm sorry. You were saying?"

He repeated the request rather impatiently. Eliza suppressed a sigh and acquiesced.

The other passengers from the wrecked stage were straggling into the courtyard. Mr. Slaughter gave his coat a vigorous shake and shrugged it on over his bare torso, then they followed the others inside.

Eliza tried to ignore the strange looks she and her "brother" were receiving. As if it weren't bad enough that by now all of the coach passengers would have heard that Mr. Slaughter was an ex-convict, the other folk in the crowded public room were gaping at his sartorial peculiarity. He, however, walked up to the plump-cheeked barmaid with all the aplomb of a Brummel who'd spent the entire morning perfecting his toilette. After a bit of haggling he turned to Eliza. "A shilling, please." She dug into her reticule and handed him the coin with a speaking look.

The barmaid, who was also the landlord's wife, excused herself and was gone but a moment, during which Eliza stood self-consciously on first one foot and then the other, all too aware of the attention focused on them.

"It's clean, anyways," the barmaid informed the

ex-convict on her return. She thrust a coarsely woven, smocklike garment toward him.

"Perfect," he said, smiling, as he shrugged out of his squalid superfine coat there before the entire assembly and put Eliza even further to the blush. The smock ballooned around him. "A portly gentleman, your husband, I take it." He grinned.

The barmaid giggled. "Pig-fat, you could say." Then she sobered up and returned to business. "You did say as how you'd throw in your coat as well." Mr. Slaughter gingerly picked the garment up off the floor. She threw it underneath the counter, wiped her hands upon her apron, and turned to wait on the sullen coachman, who was demanding tea.

"Well, Miss Osborne, do I now meet with your approval? Silly question. Let me amend it. Do I at least have a better air about me?"

"It's an improvement. And now that you've bathed and dressed in front of me and the rest of the world, do you think you might find out when we can be on our way?"

She crossed the room to take a seat on the settle by the empty fireplace while he consulted with the coachman. He soon joined her. "I'm afraid it isn't good news." He sighed. "An axle's broken. And the wheel's a total loss. We'll be here a while."

"Oh, dear." She looked stricken. "Surely not overnight."

"Shouldn't think so. Stays light forever this time of year, you know. Afraid your aunt will worry?"

"Well, n-no. Not exactly."

"She doesn't know you're coming, does she?" he deduced. "Well, then, no need to fret yourself. Just make the best of a bad matter. And, ah, speaking of that—I hate to bring up the subject of your reticule again, but do you think you might stand for coffee? And some buns wouldn't be a bad idea. You can still afford it."

"Were you perhaps a clerk in your, uh, previous

life?" she inquired sweetly as she fished in her purse once more. "You certainly keep a good account of my dwindling funds." It occurred to her that embezzlement might possibly have been his crime.

"No, no. Nothing like that. It's prudent to keep track. I certainly wouldn't want to live beyond your means." Then he grinned and went off for refreshments.

After a long silence during which they disposed of the buns and coffee, she remarked, "I must admit I feel better." Though ravenous, she'd taken only one of the half-dozen buns he'd ordered, recalling all too vividly the prominence of his ribs.

"Eh, what's that? Oh, yes, I certainly feel much better myself." He patted the smock billowing over his flat stomach while his eyes remained speculatively fixed on the three refugees from the top of their coach who'd gathered around a table near the bar. They were entertaining themselves by rolling a pair of dice back and forth upon the well-worn surface.

"Now there's a capital notion," Mr. Slaughter murmured. "I'd call that a civilized way to pass the time."

"Civilized!" Miss Osborne sniffed. "I've never heard that gaming signified an advanced culture."

"You haven't? Well, it does, I assure you. A branch of science, you might even say."

"*You* might say. Even I know enough to realize that there's nothing scientific about risking your money on whichever sides a pair of dice will finally wind up after you rattle and bounce them about a bit."

"Well, that's certainly one way to describe the game of hazard, though the description might come as a shock to the gentlemen in Brooks's or White's or any of the other fashionable gaming clubs."

"Just because gambling is fashionable doesn't

mean it's not a trap for flats." Eliza was rather proud of being able to fling the insulting term back in his teeth.

"You are a clergyman's niece right enough. Now I'll grant you"—he nodded toward the table where the play had begun in earnest—"hazard *may* be a trap for flats. But if you happen to be a knowing 'un like myself"—he smiled modestly—"it's an almost sure route to being in funds. Which I'll be happy to demonstrate if you'll be so good as to stake me. I believe you have a little of your blunt left."

"No!"

Her emphatic reply caused heads to turn their way. She lowered her volume but not her indignation. "What I mean to say is, it doesn't signify how much or how little money I have left. I'm not going to give it to you to gamble away. And please do not point out to me again that I would have lost it all if you hadn't tackled Gentleman Jack. For, frankly, I see no difference between being robbed by him or robbed by you."

"The difference, Miss Osborne, is that I will not be robbing you. You will be investing your funds, don't you see, with an almost sure prospect of a sizable, swift return."

"Fustian!"

"No it isn't. The problem is," he continued politely, "you don't have the slightest notion of the scientific principles involved in the game of hazard. This is also true, fortunately, of most people who play the game—like those coves over there, let's hope. And that's why they call it gambling. But if one plays the game scientifically and isn't dogged by the foulest of luck, well, really, it's just like doing one's sums at school. There's very little 'hazard' involved at all."

This sniff was eloquent.

"No, really. Let me try to explain. The important thing is, you see, to have a firm grasp of the odds.

These never change, you know. To give you one example, you have six chances in thirty-six of throwing a seven, but only three chances in thirty-six of throwing a four. Then, for another, if you have a main of seven and a chance of four, the odds are two to one against you. But with proper hedging it's actually possible to ensure—"

"Oh, do stop it!" Miss Osborne had clapped her hands over her ears. "I haven't the slightest notion of what you're talking about, nor do I care to have. You're merely succeeding in making my head spin."

"I'm simply trying to explain that it's possible to play a game of chance intelligently and—almost—be assured of winning."

"Almost!"

"Well, there's no sure thing in life. It's all a game of chance."

Eliza certainly didn't need him to tell her that. For if she'd ever been in doubt about life's vicissitudes, this day had provided ample illustration.

"I'm only asking for a small stake. And, win or lose, you'll eventually get your money back."

She sighed, then capitulated. "It's better than being prosed to death, I suppose," she muttered ungraciously as she dug into her reticule and dredged out her final coins. "There's no need to remind you that this is all I—*we*—have in the world since you've calculated that down to the last penny. But do run along and enjoy yourself."

"Thank you." He grinned. "I wonder if this is what it's like to be married."

She refused his invitation to come watch, trying to give the impression that she considered this activity beneath contempt and would find it tedious in the extreme to be a spectator. The truth was, she was not nearly so cavalier as she'd pretended to be about losing the last of her money. It was bad enough to arrive unannounced on her aunt and uncle's doorstep. But to arrive penniless as well really did not bear thinking on.

She did, however, think on it. And as she did so, she stole many an anxious glance across the room. More than once in doing so she happened to catch Mr. Slaughter's eye. But each time she looked away quickly, trying not to betray her interest.

The worst part was, she hadn't the slightest clue as to how the game was going. Certainly not from watching Mr. Slaughter's face, for it remained impassive. And while the other players were far more animated and forthcoming, they had lapsed into what might just as well have been a foreign language. Their frequent cries of "Crabs!" and "Nicked it!" were unintelligible. "Threw out" had a decidedly ominous ring, of course, but she was unable, due to distance and the fact that a curious crowd had begun to collect around the table, to tell to whom the term applied. She did hope it was not Mr. Slaughter.

Her anxieties had reached fever-pitch when their coachman stuck his head inside the door and whooped, "Brighton stage, repaired and ready!"

Eliza stood and started toward the door, reminding herself that she and the gallows-bird were not actually together and whatever he'd just done or failed to do was largely a matter of indifference.

"Oh, sister! Wait up there, will you?"

She halted in the doorway, longing to throttle Mr. Slaughter for inventing such a kinship. Reluctantly she turned to look his way. Her eyes bugged. He was busily scooping up a pile of coins from the table.

"Told you he was a wrong 'un, didn't I?" one of the disgruntled punters growled as they elbowed past her. "Cheated, 'e did, or I'm a Dutchman."

"Don't be daft," his companion replied. " 'Ow could 'e? It was your own dice he was rolling, weren't it?"

Mesmerized, Miss Osborne walked over to the table where Mr. Slaughter beckoned. He was counting his ill-gotten gains. "Cleaned 'em out." He grinned wickedly. "Comes to fifty pounds. That's twenty-five for you. Not a bad investment, now admit it. Actually beats putting your money on the 'change."

It took every ounce of Miss Osborne's mustered willpower to resist such riches. She somehow managed to refuse all but the exact sum she'd lent him. "Very well," he said, shrugging, as he counted it out. "I don't wish to violate your principles. You do have my everlasting gratitude as well. For what that's worth."

"I am a bit curious about one thing," she said as she restocked her reticule. "If Gentleman Jack and I hadn't come along, just how *did* you plan to pay your fare?" The question had been innocent enough, but suddenly she was sorry that she'd asked it.

"I wasn't planning to pick someone's pocket, if that's what you're thinking," he said dryly.

"I wasn't thinking anything."

"Oh, no? Well, then, to answer your question, the coachman who usually drives this route is a friend of mine and would have taken me aboard on credit. Unfortunately, he's ill. I was looking for someone else to put the touch to. You and Jack were rather a godsend."

As they jammed themselves back inside the coach, Eliza had to admit to herself that it was a very pleasant circumstance to be solvent once again. Now if she could only remain in charge of her funds this time. Well, she and her "banker" would soon be parting, and she'd certainly be alert for cutpurses from now on. Would Brighton be as evil a place as London? This thought brought on a brand-new worry. They'd lost two hours because of the accident. It was bound to be dark before she arrived.

The man beside her seemed to sense her anxiety. "How did you plan to get to the vicarage?" he asked.

"I'd hoped to hire someone in Brighton to take me back there. A cart, perhaps. Or something."

"Sounds rather vague to me. And how did you expect to manage with your money gone?" For a person with his shady background, he sounded unnecessarily disapproving.

"Well, I didn't expect to lose my money—twice—now did I?"

"Don't turn waspish. Now here's what I plan to do. There's a point in the road up ahead where it's not much more than five miles cross-country to Claxton. I plan to get out there and walk it. You're welcome to come with me."

She reluctantly assented. He leaned across her—this time it wasn't necessary to clap a handkerchief to her nose—and shouted instructions out the window to the coachman.

Some thirty minutes later, that worthy, now stone sober, reined in his four horses and let them out. They stood by the side of the road as the coach pulled away with a blast of the horn and a din of whistles, catcalls, and rude remarks from the roof passengers who had been fleeced by Mr. Slaughter.

"I think they know I'm not your sister," Miss Osborne observed as her ears reddened.

"Well, it's not a relationship you'd be proud of, is it?"

"It's preferable to the one they just implied."

"Well, yes, I expect so. But don't worry about it. You'll never see that lot again. Come on. Let's get you to the vicarage."

He took her elbow to help her over the stile that led to an apple orchard.

"Why, where's the road?"

"What road? I said cross-country, remember?"

"But I expected at least a path."

"Did you now? Well, trust me. I grew up in these parts. There's no stone for miles around that I don't know personally."

And there was no stone for miles around that she hadn't stepped on, Eliza concluded as she limped into the outskirts of the tiny village of Claxton, having arrived on its cobbled thoroughfare after being lifted across a hedgerow that her companion still had the strength to jump. Dusk was falling fast. She had no heart to drink in her surroundings, only sparing a few glances for the cottages, the village shop, and the blacksmith's before she spied the square-towered stone church appropriately situated upon an eminence in the otherwise flat landscape. Just below it stood an ivy-walled rectangular house built of the same pale stone.

"That's the vicarage," Mr. Slaughter pointed out unnecessarily.

Eliza was filled with apprehension as they approached the gate. She pointedly thanked her companion formally for his escort and bade him a good evening. His jaw set stubbornly. "I'll wait here and see you safely in."

The gravel pathway that led to the green front door was only a few yards long, but it seemed like a mile and gave Miss Osborne ample time to review the impropriety of what she'd done. That Aunt Hester would be amazed to see her went without saying. But whether the initial surprise would turn to joy or dismay was now the burning question.

But in point of fact, her aunt chose neither of these alternatives. For when Mrs. Tomkins herself, small, plump, and comfortable-looking, answered the door in response to Miss Osborne's rather timid knock, she hardly spared a glance for her favorite niece. Her eyes had traveled down the gravel path to the tall figure standing by the gate in the gloom.

Her mouth flew open and her eyes grew wide. "Oh, dear heaven, it can't be!" she exclaimed in a

25

startled whisper to the world at large. "Yes, I do believe it is. That's Garrick Slaughter, sure enough. He's actually come back to Claxton. May the saints preserve us!"

Chapter Four

"**A** *thief!*"

Eliza stared at her Aunt Hester with disbelief. The two of them were sharing a pot of tea in the vicarage drawing room. Her uncle had excused himself after dinner to retire to his study and work on next Sunday's sermon.

It may have been that the Reverend Tomkins had already become engrossed in his homily since he had seemed to find nothing at all odd in the fact that his wife's niece had turned up so unexpectedly. He had shaken his head and clucked his tongue a bit when he learned that she'd been accompanied by Mr. Slaughter. But the reaction seemed more in sorrow than in condemnation of her conduct. Mr. Slaughter, and not Eliza, appeared to be the subject of his thoughts.

Apparently both the vicar and his wife accepted the edited version of her adventures. For without

27

precisely saying so, Eliza somehow managed to convey the impression that her only contact with Mr. Slaughter was when he'd volunteered to guide her in a shortcut after he'd learned her destination was the same as his.

"Yes, m'dear," Mrs. Tomkins was now saying, "a thief. I don't wonder that you're shocked. Believe me, no one was more aghast than I when the story first came out. For a more delightful lad you could not imagine. And honorable. I would stake my life on that. Oh, he was mischievous, of course. But then what lad worth his salt is not? I simply cannot think what happened. I collect that the temptations of the city must have proved too much. He ran with a worldly crowd, I understand. Corinthians, I believe they call them. Or is it bucks? Anyhow, I was given to understand that his friends were the most tonnish of the ton. 'Vanity of vanities, saith the Preacher.'" She shook her head sadly and pushed a lock of brown hair, still untouched by gray, back up into the prison of her ruffled cap.

"But a thief! I would never have believed it."

"Of course you wouldn't," her aunt said sympathetically. "And I'm not blaming you at all for accepting his offer of an escort. For in spite of everything he must still appear very much the gentleman, though it did seem he was dressed a little oddly. Of course it was rather dark and I couldn't see him well. Besides, for all I know, that sort of thing may be all the crack in London. That Brummell person could be up to one of his queer starts again. No, I can see that you were probably grateful for his protection. And I don't wish to pry, dear, but it does seem rather odd that you were traveling alone—and on the public stage."

Eliza had been steeling herself to explain that very thing, but as she opened her mouth to do so, her aunt reverted to the subject of Mr. Slaughter. She should be grateful, she supposed, that this infamous gentleman had diverted so much attention from herself.

"You do understand, don't you, Eliza, that in the ordinary way of things I'm not a gossip-monger. For Mr. Tomkins says a vicar's wife must be above such things. But it wouldn't do *not* to tell you of the scandal since you've actually become acquainted with Mr. Slaughter. And I shouldn't wonder if you didn't find him most attractive. I certainly would have done so at your age. And if all that terrible business hadn't happened, why, I do believe that in spite of what dear Mr. Tomkins might think of such bold conduct, I would be tempted to throw you at Mr. Slaughter's head. His antecedents were a bit— well, *unconventional*, let us say—but he was always accepted here. And as I just said, he was part of the fashionable world in London. In fact, they say that he was about to make a brilliant match. But now, of course—"

"Aunt Hester!" Eliza raised her voice and stemmed the flow. "Please tell me. What did Mr. Slaughter steal?"

"I'm getting to that, m'dear," she chided. "You see, I'd just concluded that I'd best back up and give you the whole of the young man's history. It's not gossiping to do so. I think even Mr. Tomkins would have to admit as much, though I'd prefer that you not tell him that I've done so. But after all, what I'm about to say is common knowledge. And it will be much better that you know the facts, for we're certain to be asked to the Hall during your visit here. And ignorance could plunge you into the most awkward of situations."

Eliza was beginning to understand why her father was prone to refer to his youngest sister as "that rattle" and to say that it was one of life's greatest mysteries how a pretty, lively girl with many matrimonial chances had wound up marrying a clergyman, and a poor one at that. But Eliza had no inclination to stem the tide. For the truth was, she was dying to hear as much as possible of Mr. Slaughter's history. She snapped back from woolgathering to see that her aunt was looking at her expectantly. "Oh, do please go on," she said.

"Well, the first thing you must know—since it's never been kept a secret, though a newcomer to the village might, of course, think of him as the good doctor's son since that is the name he goes by, of course, though he was never legally adopted, his lordship wouldn't hear of it, I'm told—is that Garrick Slaughter is actually Lord Wenham's natural son."

"You mean he's a bastard?"

"Eliza!" Mrs. Tomkins's pretty face frowned her disapproval.

"Oh, I am sorry. Do forgive my plain speaking." It just went to show how one day in the wrong company could erode one's standards, Eliza thought. "It's all such a huge shock. I actually meant to say 'illegitimate.' "

"That does sound less harsh, I must agree. But in either case, Garrick Slaughter is the result, so I'm told, of a liaison his lordship had with a concert singer back in his youth.

"It's difficult nowadays to imagine Lord Wenham ever sowing wild oats. But the living proof of that sad state of affairs grew up right here in our village. For the unfortunate young singer died in childbirth, you see. And I don't care what others say, I believe his lordship did the proper thing when he brought the child here to Claxton. He gave the baby to Dr. Slaughter and his wife to rear. They were childless, don't you see, and doted on the lad. I'm only thankful they had both gone on to their rewards before young Garrick was sent to prison. For if they hadn't been dead already, I'm convinced it would have killed them."

Since she had paused to think over that sad possibility, Eliza gently prodded once more. "You have yet to tell me, Aunt Hester, what it was he stole."

"A pair of diamond earrings. Very valuable, besides having been in Lady Wenham's family for simply ages."

"He stole from Lady Wenham!"

"That's right. It all happened in London, actually. He'd been to see Lord Wenham on a business matter, so I'm told, and right after he'd left, her ladyship noticed that the jewelry was missing. I don't think she suspected Mr. Slaughter for a minute, though, when she called in Bow Street. But the Runners evidently didn't believe in leaving any stone unturned, for the next day they searched Garrick Slaughter's rooms and found the jewels in his greatcoat pocket."

Mrs. Tomkins sighed deeply. Her usually cheerful face looked pained. "I can't help but believe there were extenuating circumstances. Garrick was intoxicated, for one thing. Not that that deplorable condition should be given as an excuse. But there's no denying that strong spirits cloud judgment, and he was possibly thinking that he had a right to some of the family wealth. It must have been quite difficult, when you stop to think on it, growing up in the shadow of the Hall, as it were, and knowing you were the firstborn yet unentitled to anything. But if young Garrick felt any resentment, you would never have known it. He really appeared to be a most lighthearted youth. But as Mr. Tomkins is fond of saying, who can read the mind's construction from the face—or words to that effect. Still, if that was the way that Garrick Slaughter's mind was working—that he had a right to family property, I mean to say—it's a pity he didn't help himself to something of his lordship's.

"I might as well go on and say, Eliza, that many of the folks around here held it against her ladyship that she didn't just let the matter drop when her earrings were found in Mr. Slaughter's pocket. But perhaps matters had gone too far by then. After all, once she'd reported that they'd been stolen, it was a little late to pretend they'd been a gift. But it was a known fact that her ladyship deeply resented having her husband's love child constantly flung in her teeth, as you might say. And it couldn't have helped matters at all that her son seemed like an imperfect copy of the other. Anyhow, Garrick was arrested, tried for theft, and put in prison." She sighed once more. "Still, his sentence wasn't as harsh as it might have been, I'm told."

A thief. Eliza experienced a rush of emotion that she found difficult to define. Disgust would have been appropriate, but what she was feeling was more like disappointment. Or even sadness. She'd known from the start, of course, that Mr. Slaughter was a criminal. But she'd envisioned a more romantic sort of crime. Something swashbuckling would suit him. "Stand and deliver!" sprang instantly to mind. But a thief! Stealing was so sordid . . . so pedestrian . . . so *common*. Wasn't that the usual term, a *common* thief?

It was hard to believe that Mr. Garrick Slaughter, he of the cool blue eyes, was actually no better than Gentleman Jack Oliver who'd lifted her reticule. Really, this had been the most dreadful day. It was unbelievable how trusting and naïve she'd been when she'd left home at dawn and how worldly wise and cynical one day's journey on the public coach had made her. Little wonder that the gentry frowned on that conveyance.

Her aunt's mind seemed to have arrived at her journey as well. "You do know, of course," she said gently, "that nothing could delight your uncle and me more than receiving a visit from you. But I must own I'm surprised by the suddenness of it. And even more so by the manner of your arrival. My dear brother was always such a stickler for propriety that I'm amazed he'd allow his daughter to travel alone on the public coach. I can only conclude that his new bride has put his head in the clouds and he can't be thinking properly."

"Papa knows nothing of my decision to come here. Well, he does by now, I collect, for they were due to arrive back from their honeymoon this evening and I did leave him a note."

"I see." The vicar's wife put down her teacup to go to the worktable and fetch some needlework. As she settled back in her chair and began to sort threads, it was obvious she was waiting for further explanation. She gave her niece an encouraging smile.

The other squirmed. "The thing is, Aunt Hester, that I rather led Papa to believe that you'd invited me here and that I'd made the trip in the company of Mrs. Keating, the postman's wife. I did ride with her as far as London," she said defensively. "It was only half a whisker."

"I see," Mrs. Tomkins repeated. "Well, as to the first part of your fabrication, you do know that you have an open invitation, so I see little harm in what you wrote. But the latter is more serious, as I'm sure you now realize. But I'm also sure you'll never do such a rackety thing again and, thank goodness, there's no harm done."

No harm done? The vision of a naked torso under the inn-yard pump reappeared to overset Eliza.

"The thing we need to talk about in order to clear the air, my dear, is why you chose to behave in such a peculiar fashion. It isn't at all like you," Mrs. Tomkins chided gently. "And I feel I needs must say that while it's understandable if you're upset over your father's marriage, really, my love, you should feel happy for him. Your dear mama has been gone what—almost three years now?" Eliza nodded. "So there's no question of dishonoring her memory. You don't dislike your new stepmama, do you?"

"N-no." In spite of her father's contrary opinion, it occurred to Eliza that her aunt was well qualified to be a clergyman's wife. The guileless gray eyes forced her to express feelings that she'd tried to hide even from herself. "Regina's years younger than Papa is," she blurted out. "Barely thirty. And she does seem awfully . . . silly. For that matter, so does Papa."

Mrs. Tomkins chuckled. "Charles acting silly? I own I'd give a monkey to see that. But never mind. They're simply in the first throes of being in love. Your stepmama may turn out to be quite sensible after all."

"You think so?" Eliza sounded doubtful. "But my liking or not liking Regina isn't the real problem. The thing is, you see, that I'm in the way. Superfluous. And they want me . . . settled."

"Well, my dear, it's only natural that your father wishes you to make a good match. What papa wouldn't? As for being in the way—"

"Oh, you don't understand, Aunt Hester." The words came tumbling out in a rush now. "They had worked it out before they left on their wedding trip. They'd been throwing Regina's brother at my head, don't you see. He's a widower. With two children. And his estate marches with ours. He's quite well off. And I l-loathe him." Tears were welling in her eyes.

"Did you explain all this to Charles?"

"I tried to. Not in such strong terms, of course. But he's so smitten that he thinks we should all be just one big happy family. He looked positively hurt when I objected. And he implied that I was jealous of Regina and therefore prejudiced against her brother."

"Well, do you suppose there might be a bit of truth there?" Mrs. Tomkins bit off a thread.

"No! Well," Eliza qualified, "I'll admit to the jealousy. But as for Mr. Cox, the man is odious, no matter who's his sister. And the thing is, you see, he offered for me the day before yesterday and I refused him. And I knew that there'd be a dreadful scene when the bride and groom came home, with Papa hurt and Regina resentful. And, well, I simply couldn't face it. I know it's cowardly, but I felt I had to get away."

Her aunt nodded. "Yes, I can understand your feelings. And as for cowardly, let's just call it prudent to give the newlyweds time to adjust to the situation and settle in comfortably together. For once the honeymoon is over, even the most doting of couples have a lot of adjusting to do. And Charles was always set in his ways. I do think you were quite wise to come here, my dear."

Eliza took a sip of her tea, which had grown quite cold during the evening's revelations, and thought what a very comfortable person her aunt was.

The latter had her lips pursed thoughtfully. "Do you know what would be the very thing?" she mused aloud. "The solution to everything? Why, to find a suitable young man for you here in Sussex. What a shame that Mr. Slaughter has disgraced himself, for one could wink at his illegitimacy. There's no use dwelling on him, however.

"Let's see now. Hmmm. Squire Robinson's son. He's a bit spotty, but he'll soon outgrow it. Oh, this will be fun!" She beamed. "Do you know, I've always longed for a daughter of my own. Who else now? What a shame George doesn't have a curate. They're such a convenience at times like this. Well, now, there's Mr. Samuel Lowe for another. Do you object to widowers on principle or was it only Mr. Cox you took exception to?

"The real catch around these parts, of course, is the Honorable Jervis Wenham, his lordship's heir. And, actually, he's not so far above your touch as some might think. Your father has been honored with a knighthood. And we are related to a baron, though only distantly. And of course dear George is a cousin to his lordship. So it would not be an unthinkable alliance. But," she said, sighing heavily, "there's no use dreaming up that sort of Cinderella story, for Lady Wenham would never countenance it. She's always kept a tight rein on her son and has her heart set on his making a brilliant match. It's no secret that she's throwing a titled young lady at his head. No, Lady Wenham would never allow you to upset her plans. It's a pity, for I do believe you two would suit."

Dear Aunt Hester, Eliza thought, smiling to herself, thinking she could ensnare the local nabob if only his mother weren't so possessive. Her aunt's attitude was a pleasant contrast to another opinion she'd recently encountered on the same subject. What had he said? That she'd be a fool to set her cap in that direction since some unknown beauty had her hopelessly outclassed.

She went on to recall the bitterness with which the gentleman in question had spoken of this lady. But then Eliza took herself firmly in hand. For after this highly educational day, if there was one thing she was determined to nip in the bud, it was any tendency she might be developing to dwell on the disgraced Mr. Garrick Slaughter. Instead, she struggled to stifle a yawn and was quite grateful when her aunt suggested that they go to bed.

Chapter Five

*T*wo days later, Eliza was eager to explore the countryside. She had quite recovered from the rigors of her journey and was ready to forget the reason for her precipitate visit and enjoy it to the full. She was particularly looking forward to seeing Warleigh Hall, which, according to her aunt, was the showplace of the area.

A servant had been sent to Brighton for her box. She dug out the sketchbook she'd remembered to pack in order to record her travels. Then, after being assured for the third time that her help was not needed in the jam-making, that in fact her aunt and Betty were so accustomed to working in tandem that she would only be in the way, Eliza set forth with all the anticipation of the most avid tourist.

The day was fine. She gazed at the azure sky with a countrywoman's keen appreciation. The bright

sun rays nipped in the bud any temptation to remove her bonnet and let the soft breeze that was
blowing ruffle her hair. It would not do to allow her
skin to darken. Though as to that, she didn't see
why such a natural thing should be thought un-
ladylike.

She had no difficulty in finding the path her aunt
had told her of, which led off the lane toward an
open meadow that would provide a view of the Hall.
She had walked three-quarters of a mile, she
judged, when, having topped a slight rise, she spied
it in the distance. "Oh, how grand!" she breathed
as she stood stock-still to drink in the sight.

She was gazing at an imposing stone structure
built in the Palladian style. Twin curves of bannis-
tered marble steps swept up majestically in front of
the rustic. The first-floor entryway was topped by a
four-columned frontispiece. Above this, a recessed
attic story was crowned with a magnificent dome.
And in front of all this grandeur a fountain played
in the midst of a reflecting pool.

I must have a picture, Eliza decided. I'll never be
able to describe this adequately to Papa. And to
Regina. At the afterthought of her new mama, Eliza
inadvertently wrinkled up her nose.

The path that she'd been following had for some
time now been skirting a stone wall. To her artist's
eye it was quite apparent that the meadow just beyond would offer a perfect vista. After a quick look
around to be sure that there was no one to observe
such hoydenish behavior, Eliza hitched up her
skirts and climbed over it.

"This really is much better." She sat down in the
long grass. The terrain sloped gently upward, till
in the distance it became a park with a broad, tree-
lined grassy expanse that directed the eye to the
magnificent dwelling that topped the rise.

Eliza studied the view with intense appreciation
before setting to work to reproduce it with her pen-

cils. If I do this well enough, she thought happily as her sketch developed, I'll do a watercolor from it. And then I'll give it to my aunt in gratitude for her hospitality. Still, though, Aunt Hester has the genuine article at hand to look at any time she wishes. It might be a nicer gesture to present it to Regina when I go back home. Eliza felt smugly righteous at having overcome her baser nature to this degree and applied herself with diligence to produce a masterpiece of reconciliation.

Except for acknowledging their presence when she scaled the wall and as a result watching carefully where she put her feet, Eliza had paid little heed to the cows that were grazing in the meadow. And she had become much too absorbed with her drawing to notice them cropping their way nearer. But now one art-loving bovine seemed inclined to peer curiously over her shoulder.

"Shoo, cow!" She waved the sketchbook back over her shoulder underneath the intruder's nose, then turned and gasped with horror. The enormous, white-faced red bull at first looked merely puzzled, but his mood changed quickly. He lowered his head, pawed the earth, and snorted.

Quicker than thought, Eliza scrambled to her feet, dropped her sketchbook, and streaked for the nearest tree. She might well have set the record for short-distance sprinting.

She had not climbed a tree since she was twelve and was relieved to discover that she hadn't quite lost the knack, though there was one bad moment when she was held fast as sprigged muslin ran afoul of a broken branch end.

The bull bellowed forth a challenge as he thundered past the elm just below the soles of her drawn-up feet. The earth shook from the impact of flesh and bone and sinew. Then, having triumphantly routed the pesky creature that had flapped its wings beneath his nose ring, the bull lost interest and began to crop the grass contentedly, unfortunately only a few yards from Eliza's tree.

Miss Osborne sat. She eyed the bull from her precarious limb-perch and tried to assess its mood. She then eyed the rocky wall and tried to assess its distance. She looked down at her sketchbook lying on the grass and hoped the bull would not trample it—or worse.

She tried her best to be philosophical. Nothing was forever. The patch of grass the bull was masticating would eventually be consumed. Or it might develop a *tendre* for the most distant cow. Or darkness would eventually fall and there must be a barn somewhere that the herd would head for, though her nemesis would certainly not need milking. Or someone might come along and rescue her. Someone might come along!

At first she thought the hoofbeats mere imagination, wishful thinking pounding in her ears. But, miracle of miracles, a rider was actually coming along the path outside the wall, with a large dog loping at his horse's hooves. Eliza wasted no time in giving tongue. "Help! Help!" she screamed.

Out of the corner of her eye she saw the bull raise its head and stare her way. Until she shrieked she must have slipped its mind. Now it snorted ominously in answer. Eliza increased her volume.

At first the rider seemed oblivious, lost in his own thoughts. "Oh, do stop!" the elm tree entreated, and the horseman, understandably startled, reined in.

"What's the matter?" he called.

Eliza considered this a stupid question and said so. She might not have been quite so forthcoming but for a case of mistaken identity. At first glance she'd taken the rider to be Mr. Slaughter and she certainly was not going to stand on points with him. She immediately realized her error, however, when the young man replied in a toplofty tone, "Instead of calling my intelligence into account, miss, you might better explain why you're trespassing on my estate."

Well, that certainly cleared up all the confusion. This, then, was the Honorable Jervis Wenham, heir to Warleigh Hall, half brother to an ex–Newgate inmate. And if he were inclined to deny that relationship—which could be a strong temptation, she collected—nature had played him a dirty trick. The resemblance between the two was striking.

Eliza now made a supreme effort to speak civilly and atone for her previous gaffe. She also tried to sidestep the issue of trespass. "I'm in your tree here," she called, "because your bull chased me up it." There was a pause while she waited for a reply. "I was rather hoping you'd come to my rescue."

"There's no need. The bull's harmless."

"Ha!" Miss Osborne's expletive earned her another stare from the suspicious bull. "That's an easy enough attitude to take from your side of the wall. *I'm* the one who was chased up this tree and, I can assure you, that animal's intent is hostile."

"So you say."

She could see his face quite clearly through the branches, and it was obvious that he didn't believe a word that she'd just uttered. "Well, for heaven's sake," she cried out in exasperation, "why on earth would I have been perched up here like some roosting fowl for the better part of an hour if I didn't know that animal has plans to trample me to a pulp the minute I come down?"

"Well, as to that," the rider sneered, "modesty prevents my saying."

"I don't see that your modesty has anything to—" she began when she pulled up short. Why, that conceited jackanapes believed she was out on this limb in order to waylay him. The branch quivered with indignation. Eliza had taken a deep breath preliminary to a tongue-lashing that just might bring the gentleman's swelled head down to normal size when the bull, who'd stopped grazing to watch the exchange, moved nearer. Discretion seemed the greater part of valor.

"You may think whatever you choose about why I'm up here as long as you get me down. So if you'll just ride beneath this limb I can drop down behind you. Even if the bull does charge, your horse should be able to outrun it. Only do hurry. That beast's coming closer." Eliza was beginning to panic once again.

"I'll do nothing of the sort. My horse objects to females."

"That's ridiculous, Mr. Wenham!" she exploded.

"Well, well, well," he jeered. "You know who I am, then, do you?"

"Let's just say your reputation for chivalry precedes you." Let him make of that anything he wished. "Now get on over here and get me down," she snapped. Her patience was wearing thin. Besides, he couldn't be much older than she was and she saw no earthly reason for deference, no matter how much he might expect it.

"I'll tell you one more time, Miss Whatever-your-name-is, that bull won't hurt you. But since you seem determined to be rescued, well, here's a knight-errant for you." He whistled to his spaniel, who had been eagerly nosing about in the undergrowth during the conversation. "Here, boy, jump!" He indicated the wall, which the dog cleared in a joyous bound. "Now go get 'im!" The spaniel sized up the situation and headed straight for the bull, barking furiously.

As Taurus turned tail, Eliza leaped from the tree and landed with a thud that sent her to her hands and knees, from which sprinter's position she pushed off and went racing across the field. She squirmed over the wall on her stomach and collapsed, panting, on the other side.

"Well done," the gentleman on the horse dryly observed.

"I do hope you aren't too fatigued by all your efforts on my behalf." Eliza found the sarcastic remark a poor representative of all the resentment she was feeling. And it certainly made no impression upon the gentleman.

"Not at all," he replied politely as she stood up and began to brush off her skirt. The sight of a triangular tear in the muslin rubbed more salt into her festering wound.

The triumphant spaniel came leaping back across the wall. "Good boy," said Mr. Wenham.

"Yes, indeed," Miss Osborne concurred as she patted the dog's head while he bounded around her trying to lick her hand. "Good boy. How delightful to find chivalry in Sussex, even if it is of the four-footed variety. Still, I collect it would be a bit much to expect you to go back and retrieve my sketchbook." She then gave the dog's master a speaking look.

She thought he was on the point of telling her to fetch the thing herself, when all of a sudden he appeared to change his mind. He dug his heels into his chestnut, wheeled it in the path, rode back some little distance, and, just as Eliza had concluded she'd seen the last of him, spun his mount and made for the stone wall, neck-or-nothing. He went sailing over it like a centaur and galloped across the field. Then in a display of skill that made Eliza gasp, he let his weight slip sideways till he defied all laws of gravity and actually scooped the sketchbook off the ground without dismounting.

"Oh, that was famous!" she exclaimed as he jumped back across the wall. She instantly regretted the spontaneous accolade that, from the disgust upon his handsome face, he mistook for flattery.

He tossed the drawing book to her without a

word. Her own polite "Thank you" was drowned out by pounding hooves.

Eliza stared after him. Astonishment at such churlishness overrode all other appropriate emotions. This state of affairs was not to last for long, however, for when a grove of trees had finally blocked him from her view, she glanced down at the sketchbook in her hand. The Honorable Jervis Wenham had ripped out her drawing of his stately home.

Chapter Six

*E*liza was fuming as she hurried toward the vicarage. "Oh, bother!" She spied a carriage pulling up before her uncle's gate. The last thing she needed at the moment was to be forced to socialize with some visitor. She had just decided to step behind a lilac bush till the caller had gone inside when the old lady being helped out of the chaise turned her way.

"Come here, miss, where I can get a closer look at you," she called out in an imperious tone. "Don't hang back so. You should learn that too much modesty is not becoming."

Eliza reluctantly approached. She'd no idea of the identity of the frail old crone who was leaning on her stick and staring her way. But from the haughty expression and the appraising manner in which the lady looked her up and down with sharp, inquisitive eyes that belied the stooped body and heavily wrinkled face, Eliza was ready to bet a monkey that this visitor was somehow related to the Honorable Jervis Wenham.

The lady's next speech confirmed it. "Just as I thought. You must be the vicar's niece. Well, I've come to tell you that if you've any notion of setting your cap for my grandson, you'd best forget it. Your uncle comes from a most inferior branch of the Wenham family, you know."

"I know nothing of the kind," Eliza was stung into replying. "But if you think for one minute that—"

"Watch your tongue, girl!" The old lady stamped her ebony cane upon the ground while the elderly coachman who supported her other arm gazed impassively off into the distance. "Don't they teach you respect for your betters where you come from?"

"They do teach us to respect our elders," Eliza retorted, letting the old harridan know just how she viewed their respective stations.

"Don't be pert. I'll have to have a word with the vicar about you."

At that moment the vicarage door flew open and Mrs. Tomkins hurried down the gravel path. "Lady Cheselden! How delightful!" To Eliza's deep disgust, her aunt came close to groveling. "I see you've just met my niece. But pray don't tire yourself by standing out here. Do come inside. I'm sorry to say the vicar's not at home. He'll be devastated that he missed you. But you will take tea, will you not, your ladyship?" With the coachman's help she ushered the old lady up the path while Eliza brought up the rear. Mrs. Tomkins's deference seemed to be having a mollifying effect, for Lady Cheselden agreed, though condescendingly, to take tea.

After they'd settled themselves in the withdrawing room and Lady Cheselden had accepted her cup and helped herself liberally to pepper cakes, she reverted to her former topic. "I was just saying to your husband's niece here, Mrs. Tomkins—"

"I beg your pardon, your ladyship, but Eliza is my niece, not Mr. Tomkins's."

"Humph! You don't say." She glared back and forth at the two relatives as though looking for a nonexistent similarity. "Well, that makes no matter. It still won't do."

"What won't do?" the vicar's wife inquired pleasantly.

"Oh, I've heard that Mr. Tomkins married above himself, but there's no use thinking that your family is any match for ours."

Even though two pink spots appeared upon her cheeks, Mrs. Tomkins's voice was unperturbed. "I'm afraid I don't quite understand. Such a comparison has never occurred to me, your ladyship."

"Of course it has." The old lady seemed to regret that she no longer held a stick to pound. "It's plain as anything. You've invited whoever's niece she is to visit you just so she can set her cap for Jervis. But she's wasting her time, as I tried to tell her."

There was a martial light in Mrs. Tomkins's usually mild eyes that Eliza had never seen before. It was suddenly imperative to head off the setdown she feared her aunt was about to deliver. For as much as she longed to send the old witch off with a flea in her ear, she was well aware that her uncle owed his living to the lady's son-in-law. It really would not do to put her in a taking.

"I can assure your ladyship," the vicar's wife had begun frigidly when her niece hastily interrupted, doing her utmost to sound civil. "What my aunt wishes to say is that since I'd never known of your grandson's existence until I came here, it's not reasonable to believe I've any designs on him."

"Most reasonable thing in the world." The visitor glared. "I wasn't born yesterday, miss. You're no different from the rest. And I can tell you that the young women of today have no shame at all. Why, Mrs. Tomkins, it would shock you to your shoe soles to know the lengths the local girls will go in order to snare a title and a fortune. Take Squire Pope's daughter, for example. The hussy was merely asked to tea, but she managed to throw herself down the stairs in order to be bedridden for two whole days—though I'll vow she was twice as sound as I was. But that fool quack Trelawney said she'd best not be moved. A carriage jolting could prove too severe, he said." She chuckled maliciously. "Wonder how many pounds the squire's wife slipped him for that medical diagnosis? But it did the scheming minx no good. Jervis didn't go near her the entire time.

"Then there was the young trollop who coaxed him out riding when she knew a storm was brewing. They were forced to take shelter in an abandoned barn. And if my daughter hadn't sent one of the grooms to look for 'em, you can well imagine the kind of starts they'd have soon got up to. Jervis may have always been a bit on the delicate side, but he's still a man, make no mistake. And his father's son. And we know only too well just what that means."

"Lady Cheselden," Mrs. Tomkins interposed, "I don't really think we should be discussing your grandson's private affairs."

Eliza could not help but regret her Aunt Hester's scruples, for she was now enjoying the outrageous old crone's babblings. She need not have concerned herself, however. Mrs. Tomkins might as well have tried to turn back the Thames as to stem Lady Cheselden in full flow.

"*Private* affairs, you say? Humph! Well, it's public knowledge that no sooner was the poor boy out of leading strings then the mamas began to plot and scheme how best to snare him. You would not believe how they throw their silly daughters at his head."

"Why, it would not surprise me at all to learn that females were dropping right out of the trees in their eagerness," said Eliza.

"Don't be pert, miss!" Her ladyship impaled Eliza with her currant eyes while the vicar's wife tried to cough away a chuckle.

"But it won't do the schemers any good." Lady Cheselden included Eliza in the classification. "For my daughter's determined to marry him off before some trollop lures him into her bed. Why, didn't his father produce a bastard when he was barely older than Jervis? And if that lightskirt he fancied himself in love with had been gentry, well, now, he'd have found himself leg-shackled, and that's a fact."

"Lady Cheselden," Mrs. Tomkins protested once again, "you really shouldn't."

"And whyever not? No use being missish just because you're married to a clergyman. It's common knowledge that Wenham's bastard grew up on our doorstep. And that's the reason Charlotte's taking steps to get her own son out of harm's way. She's picked out a proper bride for Jervis. I thought it my duty to let you know that, Mrs. Tomkins, since you've taken the trouble to invite your niece up here. It's my place to tell you it won't do the young woman any good. The matter of my grandson's marriage will soon be settled. Oh, I grant you, he ain't happy about the arrangement. Why, he went storming out of the house this very morning in a rage, saying he has no intention of marrying anybody yet. But he'll come around once he sees this young lady. She's a real beauty, so they tell me."

"A diamond of the first water?" Eliza inquired innocently.

"Precisely. She took London by storm at her come-out. Had first pick of all the beaux."

"Then you are quite sure she'll want your grandson?"

"Of course she'll want him! She may be an earl's

daughter, but when it comes right down to it she ain't all that plump in the pocket. Besides, her mother and my Charlotte were bosom bows as girls."

Lady Cheselden tarried a bit longer for a second helping of seedcake, during the consumption of which she gave the vicar's wife permission to ask her own cook for her superior recipe. Then, as she rose and brushed the crumbs from her black bombazine, she turned to face Eliza. "Do you read?" she demanded.

"Why, of course I read. I also write and do sums, though rather indifferently."

"You are far too pert for the vicarage, Miss Osborne. But never mind. I'm sure Mrs. Tomkins will take you in hand. You may come to the Hall and read to me soon. My companion does so occasionally, but her voice gets on my nerves. When it's not being pert, yours is most acceptable."

"I, uh, thank you. And I'll be happy to read to you, of course, Lady Cheselden, but," Eliza added mischievously, "aren't you afraid that if I come up to the Hall I might cast out lures for your grandson?"

"Not a bit of it. I told you that Charlotte's made her own arrangements. And Charlotte always gets her way.

"Besides"—the old lady looked Eliza up and down—"your looks may do well enough in the country where you come from. But take my word on it, you'll be no match for a titled London beauty."

All in all, Eliza concluded as she watched the crested carriage roll away, her ladyship had come off best in their verbal sparring. She turned away from the window, grateful that at least the old witch need never know she'd brought on a dismal case of the blue-devils.

Chapter Seven

Eliza had been looking forward to the Sabbath service. Not for pious reasons, she shamefully admitted to herself, but from a curiosity to see Lord Wenham's family. Her aunt's pew, she discovered, was well situated for such observation.

The folks from the Hall arrived at the last moment, as befitted their elevated station. The procession began with Lady Cheselden thump-thumping down the aisle, her stick reverberating on the flagstones and providing an impromptu fanfare. A harried-looking female of late middle age grasped the dowager's elbow. Eliza felt a pang of pity for the old harridan's companion.

She quickly turned her attention to Lady Wenham. Hers was a commanding presence: tall, slender, proud. Even as a girl she would have been described as handsome instead of pretty. Now, though her face was beginning to line and her dark hair showed streaks of gray, the term still applied.

When her eyes moved on to observe Lord Wenham, Eliza had all she could do not to gasp aloud. For it was astounding, not to say embarrassing, just how much his two sons resembled him. Even the fact that his hair was gray made little contrast to their blondness. His elder son was more like him in physique, Eliza decided, for his lordship was a bit taller and more broad-shouldered than the younger one. And when she looked quite closely, she observed that Lord Wenham was beginning to show a small potbelly and a trace of jowls. But even so, he was handsome still—a dominant male trait among the Wenhams that could almost be considered a character flaw.

As he took his seat, Jervis's eyes flickered her way with no hint of recognition in them. Eliza shot him a beaming smile just to be perverse and was gratified to see that he looked startled.

The congregation reluctantly turned its attention to the pulpit. Poor Uncle George, Eliza thought. He suffers by contrast with his distinguished patron. His plump face, crowned by the merest fringe of ginger hair, looked more cherubic than ministerial. A small man, his head and shoulders barely cleared the pulpit. He really should stand on a box, his niece concluded.

The Reverend Tomkins was well launched into the gospel lesson when Eliza felt the congregation stir. Her ears pricked at the sound of muffled gasps and murmurs. The clergyman looked startled, lost his place, and repeated his last sentence with added emphasis while he searched for it.

Beside her, Aunt Hester continued to gaze serenely up at the pulpit as though nothing untoward were going on. But Eliza was incapable of such decorum. She stole a glance back over her shoulder and her mouth flew open. Mr. Garrick Slaughter was standing just inside the sanctuary door.

Eliza ignored her aunt's gentle nudge and continued to watch as Mr. Slaughter strolled carelessly up the aisle, seemingly oblivious to the fact that he'd robbed the minister of everyone's attention. He chose a seat three rows behind his father's family pew and directly across the aisle from her. He then raised a pious face to the pulpit.

Eliza would have bet a monkey he was the only soul among the congregation to hear the sermon, which was a pity since its subject was forgiveness. She herself was far too busy stealing surreptitious glances at the latecomer to attend to its message properly.

Garrick Slaughter took her breath away. Newgate filth had been supplanted by town bronze. His coat was clearly Bond Street, bottle-green and elegantly fitted across his shoulders. His cravat was artfully arranged in some complicated fall. His collar-length hair had been neatly trimmed and swept into a Brutus. He'd lost most of his gaolhouse pallor and a great deal of his gauntness even in this short time.

Just as he'd been the last to arrive, he was the first to leave after the benediction. The folks on the pews behind hung back to give him clear passage down the aisle.

Eliza could hardly wait to get outdoors and see what had become of him. She fervently hoped that her aunt would not feel it her duty to stop and speak to all of the parishioners as they went.

She need not have concerned herself. She was not the only worshipper consumed with curiosity. As soon as Mr. Slaughter had cleared the door, there was a near stampede to get outside.

He was standing alone in the churchyard, well off the path, lighting a cigarillo. His elegant cravat might just as well have been a leper's bell. To all appearances he was quite unconcerned that not one of the folks he'd grown up amongst was making a move to greet him.

No one, that is, but the vicar's wife. Mrs. Tomkins hurried toward him with a pleased smile and an outstretched hand as if he'd just dropped in from Oxford instead of Newgate. Eliza trailed along behind her, at the same time feeling uncomfortably conscious of all the eyes upon them and enormously proud to be related to Aunt Hester.

"How nice to have you back," the vicar's wife was saying as Lord Wenham's family emerged, the last of the congregation, from the church. Lady Cheselden and her stick set the pace for their slow progression down the short flight of steps, while all eyes, with the exception of Mrs. Tomkins and Mr. Slaughter, who were deep in conversation, fixed upon them.

Breeding shows. Eliza had reluctantly acknowledged this in the sanctuary when the Wenhams were the only worshippers who had not turned to seek the source of disruption to the service. Still, perhaps there'd been no need. From the stiffening of their backs and their riveted attention to the pulpit, she suspected that they knew precisely who had entered. She was now convinced of it as the Wenhams came slowly down the steps, looking neither to the right nor to the left.

Lady Wenham's face was devoid of all expression, but a betraying muscle twitched in his lordship's rigidly clamped jaw. Like the others, Lady Cheselden stared straight ahead. The dowager could not contain herself enough, however, to head off a reverberating, eloquently disapproving sniff. Mr. Slaughter took no notice, but Eliza felt a sudden, inappropriate urge to giggle, which she struggled to subdue.

Then to the amazement of all the surreptitious watchers, the group from the manor house broke ranks. The Honorable Jervis Wenham's eyes had scanned the churchyard until they lighted on his brother. He left the family formation and started hesitatingly toward him.

Eliza had at first surmised that his slow progress was the result of indecision. Then, like a shock from one of the new, experimental electrifying machines, it struck her. Why, he's crippled. In the confines of her pew enclosure she had not been able to observe that Jervis Wenham limped heavily upon the toe of a built-up boot.

He may have been the center of all attention, but the young man seemed conscious of no one but his older look-alike. His eyes were moist as he studied his half brother's face and then embraced him. "I just heard you were back, Garrick," he said huskily. "I was coming over this afternoon. How are you? Was it . . . ghastly?"

"Well, I wouldn't recommend Newgate for a holiday," the other replied lightly, "but it wasn't too bad. I survived it, as you can see."

"Come along, Eliza." Mrs. Tomkins tugged at her niece's arm. "We must see to luncheon. Mr. Tomkins is always ravenous after the service."

As they threaded their way among the tombstones toward the vicarage, Eliza glanced back over her shoulder and saw that the brothers were still in earnest conversation, while Jervis's family waited with stony faces in their coach.

The scene was most disturbing. For if there was anything that Eliza hated, it was being made to question her own judgment. But there was no escaping that unpleasant task. Just as she'd gotten Jervis Wenham neatly characterized as a spoiled, rich, unfeeling brat, she was forced to revise her opinion and grant him a generous measure of her sincere respect. It was Gentleman Jack all over again, but this time in reverse. She couldn't be sure of anyone anymore.

Chapter
Eight

E liza *was feeling restless and at loose ends. Uncle* George was taking a well-earned nap and Aunt Hester had gone calling on a sick parishioner. There were not too many acceptable Sabbath-afternoon activities for a resident of the vicarage. She had ruled out novel-reading, which Uncle George could barely tolerate at the best of times. Nor would it be fitting to tackle the pile of mending crammed into the worktable. All in all, a walk seemed the safest option.

She was careful to set her course away from War-leigh Hall. She wanted no more contact with bulls *or* Honorables. Therefore she chose an unfamiliar dirt lane and strode rapidly along, mulling over the morning's drama, too engrossed to notice the tiny white clouds dappling the blue sky or to appreciate the scent of firs and limes.

At first she thought the figure up ahead was a

product of her imagination since he'd been uppermost in her musings. But it seemed unlikely that imagination would have changed the outfit he'd worn earlier in church for boots and buckskins. There was no limp, so it couldn't be the other one. Ergo, it must be he. "Oh, Mr. Slaughter, wait up, will you?" she called out.

He turned, a bit reluctantly, she suspected.

"There's little to do on the Sabbath besides walking, isn't there?" she remarked once she'd caught up with him. The question sounded fatuous even to her own ears.

"I'd have no problem finding other occupations. But I've developed a passion for the limitless outdoors."

"Well, yes, I collect you would have done." Eliza looked embarrassed.

"You were in church this morning and saw me sent to Coventry." He frowned down at her as he set a rapid pace. "So you must realize it will do your character little good to be seen with me."

"Oh, well, I knew that at the posting-house in London."

"Yes, but you didn't know the sordid details of my past then, did you? But by now I'll wager there's not a single skeleton left hidden in my closet."

"Well, I couldn't very well say as to that, now, could I? But," she added bluntly, "I fervently hope they've all been dragged out now."

"Sufficient then, are they?" He smiled a crooked smile. "Oh, I expect you know all. Bastard and thief. That covers it fairly well. Don't you think you'd better turn back now?"

"No. It seems rather late to turn missish after all the mileage we've put in since London. But I do wish you'd slow down a bit. Of course," she continued when he'd complied in a small degree to her request, "as you've just pointed out, one difference between London and now is that at the time I didn't know what you'd been imprisoned for. And I must confess," she confided in a rush of candor, "it came as a shock to learn that you're a thief. I'd thought of all sorts of possibilities, you see, but never that one."

"Oh, no? Well, I can assure you it's quite a popular category amongst Newgateites, so I'm surprised you overlooked it. But just what would you say, Miss Osborne, if I told you that I'm not a thief? That I did not, in fact, steal Lady Wenham's earrings?"

His tone was light and she looked up to see if he was funning. There was no humor in his intense blue gaze.

"*Are* you saying that you didn't take them?"

"Yes."

She searched his face again, then made up her mind. "Well, then, I'm forced to believe you."

He gave a dry laugh. "When the entire world, including my father and ... certain others, who I thought would have faith in me, believe I was guilty, just why are you so credulous, Miss Osborne?"

"Actually, I'm not quite sure," she answered thoughtfully. "I expect it's all a matter of character."

His laugh was more nearly genuine this time. "Oh, come, Miss Osborne. You're an abysmal judge of character. You can't have forgotten Gentleman Jack so soon."

"Well, I didn't say I thought you had a *good* character, did I?" she was nettled into snapping back. "In point of fact, I was certain that you were capable of quite a long list of wicked deeds."

"Oh, really?" He grinned. "What, for instance?"

"Murder, for instance. By duel, for choice. Kidnapping—female abduction, naturally." His eyebrows rose at that. "Highway robbery—that's technically still theft, of course, but quite a differ-

58

ent proposition from being a sneak thief. No, try as I may, I just can't imagine you ever palming Lady Wenham's jewels."

He stopped in his tracks and looked down at her intently. "You're quite serious, aren't you?"

"Oh, yes."

"Thank you," he said simply. "I should lecture you, I know, on being gullible. But right now it feels too good to find somebody with faith in me—however illogically come by—for me to try to shake it. You do know though, don't you, that when it happened I was abysmally foxed?"

"I thought you just said you weren't going to try to shake my faith. So just how castaway were you?"

"Drunk enough to go ask my father for a loan to keep a friend out of the clutches of a cent-per-center. I'd never have done that cold sober. But drunk enough to pick up some jewels and pocket them? I'll not believe it, though God knows I've had ample time to entertain the possibility."

"And have you also tried to think how they could have got into your pocket?"

His look was withering. "Just when I'd decided I'd rarely met such a wise young lady, you'd actually ask a damn-fool question like that? For God's sake, woman, I've spent the last six months thinking of little else."

"And what was your conclusion?"

"I'd rather not say."

"You mean you actually know who it was?"

"Not in the sense you mean. For I'd never be able to prove it. But when all's said and done, I only know of one person who despises me enough to do such a thing to me."

The grim set of his face persuaded Eliza to bite off her next, obvious question. "But there has to be a way to prove your innocence," she said instead.

"How idealistic you are. No, the only way I'll get my good name back is for the real culprit to confess.

And, frankly, hell will freeze over before that happens."

"You never can tell. You're always hearing of deathbed repentance."

His smile was bitter. "I'm not sure I can wait that long. No, Miss Osborne, I'm afraid it's hopeless. I was a fool to come back here. I should have done what I was told—go somewhere and start afresh."

"Don't be so defeatist. And, for goodness' sake, could we sit down a bit? You're walking my legs off again."

"Really? I am sorry. How about under that tree?" He nodded toward a spreading oak by the roadside. "Looks mossy enough not to spoil your gown."

She sank down gratefully and leaned back against the tree trunk. He followed her example, their shoulders almost touching. Such proximity put her in mind of the coach ride when his head had rested upon her shoulder and she'd been too intimidated to ask him to move it. His thoughts must have been traveling the same route, for he smiled and said, "At least I trust I smell better at the moment."

"Thank heavens."

"You know, I really do owe you an apology."

"Several probably. But no matter. As everyone points out, I did lay myself open to certain liberties by traveling alone."

"I wasn't referring to that sort of thing. I'd just like to retract something I said during our first meeting. For as I recall, I implied that you were no match for . . . a certain female."

"Actually, you didn't imply it. You stated it baldly."

"Well, I was wrong to have done so." He was studying her intently, as though really seeing her for the very first time. "You may not be quite as devastatingly beautiful, but you are most desirable, you know."

She was not entirely oblivious of his intention. But she was too astonished by it to put up any defense—even if she'd wished to do so, which remained a moot point upon lengthy reflection during the days to come. His kiss belonged to an entirely different category than the few chaste male busses she'd previously experienced. It was almost as pleasurable as it was disturbing. It left her gasping for breath, or so she supposed.

"Damnation!"

"Well, thank you very much. I know I'm hardly as experienced as you seem to be, but I'd expect a better review than that for my performance."

His laugh was genuine this time. "Eliza, in our brief acquaintance the only thing I can be sure of about you is that you will never react like any other female."

"Well, what did you expect me to do? Swoon? Slap you?"

"Oh, God, I don't know. I really didn't 'expect' anything, for I'd not the slightest intention of kissing you until it happened. And I do beg your pardon. I—"

She clapped her hand over his mouth. "I greatly fear you're going to say that you meant nothing by it, and I'd really rather you didn't. I'm already well aware that you've been shut up in prison for months now. And that you were known before as something of a rake. And Papa, when he used to preach propriety to me, did dwell on the dangers of proximity."

"Did he, indeed?" Mr. Slaughter was glaring down at her. "I realize that anything I say here can only make a bad matter worse. But if you're implying that I'd get an urge to make love to just any female who came within my range, I'll assure you I'm not that desperate. Come on." He stood and more or less pulled her to her feet. "I think we'd better walk."

They started back the way they'd come in silence. He was the one to break it.

"Look, what I was trying to say back there before I became ... diverted was that I'd sold you short. Now I'm convinced you'd be stiff competition for any female. And I'd like for you to meet my—that is, I wish you'd come to know young Jervis Wenham. The longer our acquaintance, the more I'm convinced that you'd be perfect for him. You're just the sort of woman he needs to bring him out of his shell. And, more important, out from underneath his mother's thumb."

"That certainly sounds like a Herculean task." Both her face and voice were expressionless.

"Not really. Young Jervis is coming of age, and I don't just mean in terms of the calendar. It took some backbone to defy his parents and greet me publicly the way he did. So I believe he's ready to be his own man. And to fall in love with a girl of his own choosing. I really do think that if I could contrive somehow to bring you to his attention—"

"Stop right where you are."

He obediently halted.

"Not literally." She tugged his arm and they continued. "I mean stop what you're now thinking. For I've already been brought to the Honorable Jervis's attention, you see, and the result was that we heartily dislike each other."

She then went on to relate the story of the bull, the tree, and the purloined drawing. At its conclusion he gave a heartfelt groan.

"Well, what did I just say, Eliza? That you could be depended upon to act unlike any other female. How could I have forgot so soon?"

They trudged on for a while in silence. He looked so dejected that she was sorry to have pricked his little bubble, though just why he should have his heart set on such an odd match-up was quite beyond her.

They had left the lane and were walking down the main road to the village when the sound of carriage wheels behind them snapped him out of his reverie. "Oh, God, you shouldn't be seen with me. Your reputation!"

"Well, if you're thinking of taking to your heels, forget it. That would look a great deal more odd than our walking together."

"I suppose so," he reluctantly agreed. They moved to the verge to let the carriage go by them. "Let's just hope it's no one we know."

This certainly proved true in her case. For when the open landau drew abreast, Eliza risked a glance and saw two elegantly clad ladies facing one another. The older of the two seemed to be busily lecturing the younger and did not spare the pedestrians so much as a glance. But the young lady turned her head their way and Eliza was left with a welter of impressions to contend with later on in the sanctuary of her room.

One was that the face framed by the leghorn bonnet was the loveliest she'd ever seen; another, that its expression had at first been merely curious but had instantly been transformed to shock. But the impression that overset all the rest was that the man beside her had been turned to stone.

It did not require superior deductive powers to conclude that the girl in the carriage must be the intended bride of the Honorable Jervis Wenham. And it also followed, Eliza decided, that the reason Garrick Slaughter had been so eager to throw her at his half brother's head was that he himself was in love with the golden-haired, violet-eyed vision.

Chapter Nine

*E*liza *waited impatiently for a summons to the* Hall. Not that she was eager to read to Lady Cheselden; rather, she wished to feel out the garrulous old lady on the subject of stolen jewelry.

For she was a young lady with a mission: She would get to the bottom of this mystery. The fact that she was totally convinced of Garrick Slaughter's innocence had nothing at all to do with a certain kiss. If anything, her burning desire to turn detective was an attempt to redirect her thoughts away from that disturbing occurrence.

Perhaps Mrs. Tomkins found Eliza's eagerness a bit suspect, for as her niece left the vicarage to go to the Hall she found it necessary to say, "Pray remember that Lady Cheselden is well up in years and isn't always as discreet as she should be. Nor can one rely too much upon the truth of what she says. Oh, I don't mean for a moment that she'd actually tell intentional falsehoods. It's simply that, like so many elderly people, she tends to become confused. I suppose what I'm trying to say, Eliza, is that her ladyship's tendency to reveal the private details of life in the Hall would be a source of great embarrassment to Lord and Lady Wenham if they knew of it. So do try to prevent her from gossiping if you can. And if not, pray disregard any discussions of private matters. You should realize that, odd though it seems, people tend to open up more to residents of a vicarage than to others. It's as if they think a vicar's calling is contagious." Eliza did hope so, though not without a pang of guilt.

As she followed the Wenham butler the length of a two-story hall, she caught a glimpse of the elegant saloon beyond it. She longed to stop and gawk at all its grandeur: the marble fireplace, the giltwood and figured-satin furniture, the priceless paintings that adorned the silk-lined walls. It was terrible enough, she reflected, that Garrick Slaughter was barred from such a birthright without being branded a thief as well. And someone in this household knew the truth. Eliza was convinced of it.

The butler preceded her up one of a pair of marble staircases that branched off from a common beginning at the back of the great hall. Eliza was feeling some of the zeal of a modern-day knight-errant who'd just taken up his cause. It was therefore rather disconcerting to meet one of the enemy coming down.

"Well, now. You must be our Hester's niece. Miss Osborne, is it?" Lord Wenham had paused two steps above her. This elevation, plus his impressive height, served to emphasize their respective stations. Eliza did her best to fight off intimidation. She did wish, though, that these Wenham men were less handsome. And looked less alike. The resemblance was off-putting. Still, her "Yes, your lordship" sounded fairly steady. And on the strength of that, she even summoned up a smile.

"I understand you're here to read to Lady Cheselden. It's most kind of you. For I'm sure that an attractive young lady like yourself must have many claims upon her time."

Oh, bother. Eliza was quite prepared not to like his lordship and here he was, disarmingly charming, and what's more, his face was kind. Still, he'd never been all that high up on her list of suspects, for she couldn't imagine a father deliberately sending his by-blow to prison. After exchanging a few more pleasantries, she and Lord Wenham passed each other on the stairs.

"Well, what kept you?" Lady Cheselden snapped as the butler ushered Eliza into the old lady's presence. The drawing room was filled to bursting with furniture and bric-a-brac, giving the impression that she'd clung to as much baggage from a former life as possible.

"You did say three, did you not?" Eliza asked just as the mantel clock struck that hour.

"Don't be pert!" The dowager motioned to a chair near the sofa where she was reclining. "And I suppose you're expecting tea."

"Why, no, thank you, your ladyship, I—" Eliza stopped short as it became quite evident that it was her hostess who wished refreshments. A maid had come in with a heavily laden silver tray.

After the servant had withdrawn, her ladyship fortified herself with several greedy bites of sponge cake, then went on the attack. "I intend to have a word with your aunt, miss, about her conduct. Won't do, you know. I don't care if she is a clergyman's wife. She is still your aunt. *In loco parentis.* And she has no right to expose you to slander."

"Aunt Hester? But what on earth . . ." Eliza had previously thought the old lady eccentric. Now she believed her mad. "I can assure you, ma'am, that my aunt is the soul of propriety."

"No she ain't. Not a bit of it. I saw her march right up to that gallows-bird after church was over. Well, it's one thing if some muddled notion of Christian charity made her feel that she needed to welcome that thief back—though to my way of thinking she'd've set a better example by letting it be known that folk around here won't put up with his sort. But to introduce a genteel young lady like yourself to that thieving bastard, well, it won't do, I tell you, and I intend to speak my mind to Mrs. Tomkins when I see her."

Eliza had been racking her brain all day wondering how to introduce subtly the subject of the purloined jewelry. Now it had been done for her. She tried not to look delighted. "Perhaps," she ventured, "my aunt has difficulty believing that Mr. Slaughter would do such a terrible thing."

"Not believe it!" her hostess snapped. "He's just out of Newgate, ain't he? And years too soon by my way of thinking. They should have shipped the bastard off to Botany Bay. And would've done, I'll vow, if a lot of palms hadn't been greased. Wouldn't've happened in my day, I'm here to tell you. They knew what to do with thieves back then. Hanging's the only thing."

Eliza tried not to entertain the thought of Garrick Slaughter swinging from a gibbet. "I've heard that Mr. Slaughter has many influential friends. Are you implying that one of them bribed the judge to get him a lighter sentence?"

"Influential friends." Her ladyship's lip curled. "Bunch of rackety, well-born hell-raisers, I'll call 'em. Too deep in debt themselves to dip into their pockets for Garrick Slaughter, even if they'd had the inclination once he'd shown his true colors, which I doubt. No, if there was any bribing done, and I'll wager my life on that, it's my daughter's husband who put up the blunt. He's always had a soft spot for his bastard. I tell you, Charlotte's a saint to have put up with what she has. Do you know of any other female who'd tolerate having a husband's by-blow constantly flaunted in her face?"

"Well, no, that is, at least I can't think—"

"Of course you can't! It's unheard of. And I told Charlotte from the outset that she should put her foot down and have the brat sent away somewhere. But no. She was too much in love. And too afraid of losing Wenham. So she decided just to blink at the situation. I told her plain she was a besotted fool. The idea of allowing one of the estates that should by rights belong to her own son to be willed away to that bastard. I'd not have stood for it, I can tell you."

Eliza tried not to think of her aunt's admonition against encouraging the old lady to gossip. "Lord Wenham actually did that?" she prodded.

"Don't blame you for sounding shocked, but that's exactly what he did. Happened before he and Charlotte married. Said he felt a moral obligation to the boy. Moral, my eyebrow! Call it moral to take away your legitimate son's rightful inheritance and give it to your doxy's brat? Well, at least Wenham finally had his eyes opened. Blood and breeding will tell, every time. The lightskirt was actually on the stage, you know." Lady Cheselden made this sound rather worse than prostitution. "Why, the boy's very name Garrick was after some actor cove. Well, never you mind his honors at Oxford and his ton-nish clubs and his visits to Almack's. For blood will tell. Every time. Sooner or later he was bound to show his true colors. And I, for one, am just thankful it happened in time to correct the injustice that was done to Jervis."

"You mean that his lordship has disinherited Mr. Slaughter?"

The other chuckled maliciously. "What else could

he do once the thievery had come to light? What's the world coming to when gentlemen treat the results of their dalliances the same as their lawful children? Well, then, miss, did you come up here to read or to chatter?"

Lady Cheselden's appreciation of her voice, so Eliza decided not many minutes later, must have been for its soporific qualities. For she was no more than three pages into *Humphry Clinker* when the old lady began to nod. And by page four she was snoring noisily. Eliza was in a quandary. Should she tiptoe from the room and risk incurring the old harridan's wrath later on, or should she simply sit there till her ladyship awakened, which could be a week from Tuesday judging from the timbre of the sounds she was making? It was a relief to hear footsteps hurrying down the corridor. Lady Cheselden's companion paused a moment on the threshold to catch her breath, then tiptoed toward Eliza.

"Oh, good, you're still here," she whispered. "I was afraid you'd already gone and her ladyship would be displeased that I'd left her unattended. But I had to prepare a poultice for poor Master Jervis. I was his nurse when he was a child, you see" —her plain, washed-out face grew animated at the recollection—"and a dearer little lad you cannot imagine."

She was certainly right on target there. Eliza couldn't.

"And when the poor sweet suffered so with his bad foot, there was no one like Nana to make the hurt go away. I still refuse to allow the servants to prepare my special remedy. Servants are so careless as a rule. But here I am, rattling away, and I haven't even introduced myself. I am Miss Hurst. My present position is companion to Lady Cheselden."

After a bit of whispered consultation, punctuated by her ladyship's raucous snores, it was decided that Eliza should dispense with any formal leave-taking and depend upon Miss Hurst to explain to Lady Cheselden that she was due back at the vicarage.

As she walked down the staircase, she could hear the strains of a pianoforte being played, none too skillfully. The saloon door was still open, so she risked a peek. The much-discussed diamond of the first water was seated at the instrument, playing with intense concentration, while the Honorable Jervis Wenham leaned heavily upon it. Eliza noted that there did, indeed, appear to be lines of suffering etched around the young man's mouth. But whether this was due to the fact that he was in some need of Miss Hurst's poultice or because he had an ear for music, it was impossible, of course, to say.

At that moment he glanced her way and their eyes met. She felt a rush of embarrassment and turned quickly away to hurry across the marble checkerboard to the outer door, which a powdered footman was holding open for her.

Eliza was deep in thought as she walked slowly down the tree-lined driveway that snaked its lengthy way to an iron gryphon-flanked entry gate. There was much to assimilate. Two brothers, one of whom seemed to have everything. Everything, that is, except for perfect health. And perhaps his father's favoritism. And, most important, an unentailed estate that in the normal course of things would have come to him as part of the heir's inheritance. Would those omissions be enough to cause him to destroy the other brother out of gnawing greed or jealousy?

Eliza had begun to feel like a bloodhound that just picked up a quarry's scent. Where had Jervis been when the jewelry disappeared? she wondered. And what of the other members of this household? Which ones had been in London at the fateful time?

Well, she'd have to fish for that information on her next visit, and be quick about it, before putting Lady Cheselden to sleep again with Mr. Smollett's novel.

Chapter
Ten

Whch Eliza volunteered to deliver clothing to a needy family, it seemed a good idea to take the donkey cart. This was her first experience with these perverse little beasts and she soon discovered they had minds of their own. On the way home their temperament reached its zenith. They balked in the middle of a narrow wooden bridge and refused to budge. She shouted and cracked her whip to no avail. The donkeys stubbornly retained their stationary mode.

"Oh, botheration!"

She climbed out of the cart, clasped one of the beasts by its bridle, and began to tug. Both donkeys simply set their hooves more firmly and looked at her with reproachful eyes.

"Come on, you stubborn jackasses, move!" she exhorted through clenched teeth. The distant sound of an approaching carriage made evacuation urgent. It didn't happen.

Traveling at a rapid clip, a curricle swept around a curve just beyond the bridge. It required no small skill to pull up the pair of perfectly matched grays before disaster happened.

"You could have killed us, you ninnyhammer! Get off the bridge!"

"What exactly do you think I'm trying to do?" she snapped as she gave the donkey's bridle a fearful yank. The only result was to almost part her arm from her shoulder socket.

"Don't jerk. You'll only annoy them."

"*I'll* annoy *them*!" She jerked again with the same results.

"Pull them steadily, firmly. They'll come."

And just what did he suppose she'd been doing for the past ten minutes? Eliza bit back the retort, though, and followed his advice. Nothing.

"Apply more pressure and speak to them as you do so."

"Now, really!" Her patience, if nothing else, slipped its rein and bolted. "If it's conversation these animals need, suppose you come talk to them. You seem to speak their language."

The Honorable Jervis Wenham's face flamed red while the beauty beside him giggled. Eliza wished she had bitten off her tongue. She felt even worse when he handed the reins to his companion, who went rather pale but voiced no protest, climbed down from the rig, and started toward her. His limp was more pronounced than she recalled it, and there was fury in his eyes. He doesn't want the diamond to watch him walk, she realized.

"What are you going to do?" she asked as he climbed into the cart.

"What you should have done. Drive them."

"Good luck, then," she muttered as she got back up beside him, trying not to quail before his glare.

"Just what do you call this thing?" He picked up the tiny whip she'd abandoned on the seat and eyed it scornfully. "A fly brush?"

"If you've a better instrument of torture in your rig, I'll be glad to fetch it."

Any reply he might have made was forestalled by the sound of other hoofbeats. Mr. Garrick Slaughter, mounted on a large black stallion, galloped around the bend and reined in beside the curricle.

Eliza would have wagered earlier that the nervous beauty was incapable of turning paler. She would have lost. The lady left holding the grays looked as if she might swoon at any moment. Mr. Slaughter's expression was harder to read. Just as Eliza was sure his heart was in his eyes, that remarkable blue gaze turned their way and a grin transformed his face. He'd arrived at the very moment when Jervis had risen to his feet with the ridiculous little whip brandished aloft. The young man held the pose.

"I'd heard you'd become a famous whip, Jerry." The laughing eyes drank in the balking donkeys, the donkey cart, and Miss Eliza Osborne. The grin broadened. "Thinking of applying to the Four-in-Hand Club, then, were you?" he inquired, referring to the exclusive whipsters' club of which he was a member.

"Go to the devil, Garrick." Jervis's answering grin was rather grudging.

"Bet half a crown you'll never move 'em."

"Done!"

"Hiii-yah!" Mr. Wenham gave a fearful shout and at the same time flourished the tiny whip. The latter action resulted in more *pop* than *crack*, but either the shout sufficed or for reasons peculiarly their own, the donkeys moved. In fact, the little beasts evacuated the bridge with more verve than they'd exhibited all day long. It could almost have been said that they bolted. Eliza clapped her chip straw bonnet more tightly upon her head. Her teeth were rattling.

"Y-y-you c-can s-s-stop now."

"Stop? Are you daft? After all I've been through to get them started?"

They took a bend in the road on two wheels, while Eliza clung to the seat for all she was worth. "Slow down, you idiot! This isn't a c-curricle, you know."

He gave her a taunting grin and urged the little animals onward.

But Eliza had had more than enough. She grabbed hold of the reins in front of his hands and tugged them with all her might.

"Watch what you're doing!" he commanded.

The maneuver, which coincidentally had placed her practically in his lap, was quite effective. The tired animals slowed down and soon came to a standstill under one of the elms that bordered the lane.

"And just how do you propose to get them started again?" he inquired conversationally. His ill humor seemed to have vanished.

"You don't really think your goddess back there is capable of driving your curricle, do you? Exactly how far do you wish to walk back?"

His ill humor was not given short holiday. It returned once more full force. "No need to concern yourself with my walking ability. I assure you, I can make it."

"I wasn't concerned. At least no more than I would have been for—"

"An able-bodied man?"

"My word, you're testy. I don't see why you should make such a Cheltenham tragedy over a little limp."

"I do not make a Cheltenham tragedy of it," he replied through gritted teeth.

"Yes, you do. I saw the way you reacted before your Miss Diamond of the First Water."

"Her name is Lady Juliet. And furthermore—"

"Juliet!" she choked. "You made that up! Still, what else would she be called? Guinevere, perhaps? Or Helen? But never mind all that. The point is, your attitude's absurd. Why, take Lord Byron, for example. He's made the limp romantic. I doubt the man would walk normally if he could."

"Miss Osborne, it amazes me that someone hasn't strangled you long before now."

"The subject of your limp is taboo, then? I might have known. But I can't believe you'd be any the worse for some plain speaking."

The donkeys, on their own, suddenly decided to move again. "Well, what do we do now? Do I drive you back or do you walk?"

"Neither."

"You plan to fly, perhaps? Is there a balloon around here somewhere?" She gazed pointedly all around them at the empty meadows and copses.

"I plan to remain aboard until I understand why anyone would venture out in such an absurd equipage."

"Well, I can solve that mystery for you. My uncle's living doesn't allow for carriages. Perhaps when you become viscount you might rectify the situation."

"I see." He looked almost embarrassed.

"Well, now, shall we go back? I should think the fair Juliet would be growing impatient."

"She's in good company."

Eliza frowned, trying to read his face. "Oh." The light had dawned. "I see. So that's what this is all about. You're leaving those two alone together."

"Bravo! And just when I had serious doubts about your intellect."

"Well, isn't that a trifle risky? Not many men would be so generous with their fiancées."

76

"She's not my fiancée. As a matter of fact, she and Garrick had a secret understanding before . . . his problem."

"Oh, really?" Eliza found this bit of information rather lowering. "So now you think they can patch things up?"

"I don't know. No, dammit, I don't," he muttered, more to himself than to her. "I doubt whether her father would have allowed the match to take place even before. And now—no, I don't believe there's a prayer for them. But Garrick deserves the chance to plead his case."

"Yes," she concurred. "He should at least let her know he's innocent."

"Innocent? Whatever put that maggot in your head? The diamonds were found in his possession. He was tried and convicted."

Eliza almost crowed aloud at the turn their conversation was taking. Detecting seemed to be her forte. She had the Honorable Jervis Wenham just where she wanted him. To apply a bit more pressure she impaled him with an all-knowing look. "True, Mr. Slaughter was judged guilty. But you know better, don't you?"

She was gratified to note that he turned a trifle pale. A sign of guilt if she ever saw it.

"I know nothing of the sort," he retorted. "Oh, I know he denied taking the curst things and claimed to have no notion of how they got into his pocket. And I believe him. Garrick wouldn't lie."

"But he'd steal?"

"No. Yes. I mean, of course he wouldn't in the ordinary way of things. But he was foxed, dammit. And anxious for his friend. I don't think I'll ever forgive my father for not simply giving him the money. It's not as if he'd ever asked a favor before. I think Papa might have done so if my mother hadn't been listening. But never mind all that. The point is, I expect the upshot was that in his drunken state Garrick believed he deserved better from our father and just helped himself. Then when he sobered up, he couldn't remember that he'd done so."

"Yes, that's certainly one explanation." It was not one she particularly cared for.

"The only possible one, in fact."

"Oh, I shouldn't go that far. There's always the possibility that someone else put the jewels in his pocket."

"Why would anyone do a damnable thing like that?"

"Oh, there could have been good reasons. For one, I understand that Lord Wenham has disowned him. That means another estate for you, does it not?"

For a moment she feared he was going to strike her. He certainly looked sufficiently enraged.

"You . . . you . . . loose screw! How dare you imply I'd do a thing like that to Garrick! And for a paltry estate in Hampshire. Dammit, he's my brother!"

Eliza was intimidated but not routed. "*Unacknowledged* brother, though."

"Not by me. It's none of your damn business, Miss Osborne, but I'll have you know there's no one on earth I care for more than Garrick Slaughter. Why, if it weren't for him I'd most likely be an invalid right now. You'd not believe the way my mother and Miss Hurst coddled me. But not Garrick. He used to spend all his school holidays working with our horses, and I'd pretend to be sick, lock the door, sneak out my window, then head for the stables. He not only taught me to ride and drive, he saw to it that I learned to swim. My God, he threw me in the lake over and over and over till I got rather skilled." He grinned suddenly at the recollection. "Garrick's attitude was that just because I'd never win prizes in foot races there was no reason I couldn't excel at other things. He even taught me how to box. I wasn't too good at that, of course. To really excel, you need agile footwork. But he saw to it that I could at least defend myself. I can land a punishing left if I have to."

"Yes, given your disposition, I can see where he'd consider self-defense important."

"Go to the devil, Miss Osborne." Mr. Wenham grinned once more, then quickly sobered. "Anyhow, don't accuse me of sending my brother to prison. You've maggots on the brain if you think that."

Maybe. Eliza was almost convinced that he spoke the truth. Still, it might be a case of the gentleman doth protest too much. And he'd certainly looked guilty when she first broached the subject.

He interrupted her racing thoughts. "You haven't said just what your particular interest in all this is. Besides blatant nosiness."

"Justice." She managed to sound gratifyingly top-lofty.

"Fustian." He looked at her intently, then a light slowly dawned on his frowning face. "You know Garrick, don't you?"

"Well, we have met," she admitted.

"So that's it, then. Of course. You're in love with him."

"I am not!"

"Certainly you are. Females always fall head over heels for Garrick. But you're wasting your time. If you think for one minute—" His words were suddenly cut off by a kid glove clapped roughly across his mouth.

"Mr. Wenham, pray pay attention. I am not—let me repeat it, *not*—in love with your half brother. But all the same, I think it only fair to tell you that if one more person informs me that I'm no match for that raving beauty we left back there in your curricle, well . . . well . . . there's simply no saying what I might do!"

Chapter
Eleven

*T*wo *messages arrived at the vicarage the next* morning. One was an invitation to join Lord and Lady Wenham and their houseguests for dinner that evening. The other was a letter from Sir Charles Osborne.

Eliza excused herself and took it to her room to read, away from the anxious eyes of Aunt Hester. It was even worse than she had feared. Her father came directly to the point. He was disappointed, no, *displeased*, that she had treated Mr. Cox's offer of marriage so cavalierly. Had she any notion of just how deeply she had offended, no, *hurt*, his bride, her stepmama? She had shown a lack of maturity he could not conceive of. She was aware, was she not, that she would soon turn twenty and that eligible men did not grow on trees? Mr. Cox's fortune was more than a mere competency. That, coupled with the close relationship of their two families, made him eminently suitable.

The letter ended on what was meant to be a conciliatory note. It only served to plunge her deeper into gloom. Her father had conceded that her precipitate visit might prove to be a good thing after all. For surely time and distance would give her room for reflection. He was confident Eliza would at last come to her senses and do the proper thing. What's more, he had passed these same assurances on to Mr. Cox. With greetings to his sister and her husband, he remained her most affectionate father, Charles Osborne.

All in all, it was a very good thing that Eliza could look forward to the evening at the Hall. It prevented her from becoming blue-deviled. She was a bit surprised, though, to find that her aunt's anticipation outdid her own. It made her wonder if the vicar's wife perhaps felt some regret for the social life she'd turned her back on. When her aunt came into her room for the second time that morning to check on which gown she planned to wear, Eliza was tactless enough to wonder this aloud.

"Do you really think I attach too much importance to the occasion, Eliza? I can't agree. In the first place—and I don't mind admitting to this much worldliness—it is gratifying for dear George's sake to be treated as family by his lordship. But more important, just now I'm delighted that you can have this opportunity for a bit of gaiety. We are so dull here. There's little to entertain you."

Eliza stoutly contradicted her aunt on that score and assured her that she was enjoying her stay prodigiously.

"That's nice to hear, m'dear. But all the same it would be foolish not to look upon dinner at the Hall as an opportunity. Especially in view of your father's odious letter." (Eliza had passed the letter along to her aunt to read and it had produced a surprising amount of indignation in that usually placid lady.)'' I have not forgotten my stated intention of doing a bit of matchmaking on my own.''

''But, Aunt,'' Eliza said, laughing, ''you are aware that we're being dished up as entertainment for Lady Greenwood and her gorgeous daughter. And you do know that the aforementioned gorgeous daughter is intended for the Honorable Jervis Wenham? So I fear you must strike that gentleman from your list.''

''Well, yes,'' Mrs. Tomkins acknowledged, her face reflecting some regret. ''But there could be other young gentlemen present, and the white lace over pink satin is bound to be more becoming than this spotted crape you've chosen.''

Much to Eliza's relief, they had planned to walk to Warleigh Hall, the cart and donkeys having been ruled out as somewhat lacking in dignity. But thirty minutes before the time set for their departure, a chaise pulled up before their gate. ''How kind,'' the vicar announced, peering out one of the front windows. ''His lordship has sent a carriage for us. I'll just go speak to the driver. Perhaps he'd like a cup of tea in the kitchen while he waits.''

The Reverend Mr. Tomkins quickly returned with a look of astonishment upon his face. ''Why, it's for us.''

''Of course,'' his wife replied. ''Who else at the vicarage is expected there for dinner?''

''No, no. You don't understand, m'dear. The chaise is *ours*. Not just on loan for this evening. Ours to keep. A gift from his lordship, with an apology for not having thought of the need sooner.''

''But how astounding!'' Mrs. Tomkins's eyes were wide with amazement. ''What could have made him think of such a thing just now?''

Eliza had all she could do to ward off a smirk.

Arriving in style seemed fated to be the highlight

of the evening, Eliza thought as she surveyed her fellow guests. They were seated at the long, gleaming mahogany table in the Hall's sumptuous dining room. It was fairly set ablaze with candlelight, which reflected off the highly polished crystal and silver.

Besides the vicarage party and the guests of honor, the only other guests present were an elderly couple, Sir Joshua and Lady Sloan, both hard of hearing, whose estate, it seemed, marched next to his lordship's; and a young Dr. Patterson, who not only possessed a wife but one in the family way. Eliza sent a speaking look up the table toward her aunt as if to say "What a waste of my best lace over satin."

The unfortunate doctor, seated next to Lady Cheselden, was being bombarded with a long, tedious recital of the shortcomings of his predecessor, the late Dr. Slaughter. Since this had to do in the main with the physician's mistreatment of her grandson's ailments, starting with Jervis's birth and continuing through two removes, there was little need for anyone in her ladyship's vicinity to search for topics of conversation. Eliza, directly across the table, could not help but wonder just how much of the venom in this diatribe was due to the fact that the late doctor had been the foster father of Garrick Slaughter. She also wondered how Jervis, with his overly developed sensitivity to his lameness, was taking this review of his case history.

Eliza glanced his way, feeling sympathetic. But her kindly impulse was wasted. Jervis Wenham's slightly glazed eyes were intent on the beauty seated beside him. There was a fatuous expression on the usually intelligent face as he bent to hear whatever message she was murmuring in his direction. And though his plate was liberally piled with lamb, veal, duck, and green peas, Eliza saw that he'd hardly touched it. Suppressing a sigh, she turned to address a remark to the doctor's wife in the conversational lull left while Lady Cheselden masticated a large mouthful of food. But just as Eliza was about to make her comment, her ladyship was off again with a detailed description of little Jervis's migraines.

All in all it was a blessed relief when dinner was over and Lady Wenham finally signaled that the ladies would leave the gentlemen with their port.

Eliza lurked near the entrance to the drawing room until Lady Cheselden had found a seat. She then made for a settee as far from that grande dame as the social situation would allow. She had had more than her fill of her ladyship's monologues.

To her surprise, Lady Juliet also crossed the room and sat beside her. "Aren't you the young lady with the donkey cart?" she asked, dimpling at the memory. Eliza was now able to observe closely, and with a tiny twinge of jealousy, how very appealing the goddess was.

"Yes, I am," she admitted. "And I should beg your pardon for all the inconveniences I caused you."

"Not at all. I vow I don't know when I've been so diverted. Donkeys are the oddest creatures, are they not? It was so comical to watch Jervis treating them like rare bits of blood."

"Yes, he certainly looked a nonesuch." Eliza chuckled at the recollection. Then, because she couldn't hold her curiosity in check a minute longer, she ventured, "At least you were given the opportunity to have a private conversation with Mr. Slaughter."

Much to her amazement, the beauty turned a fiery red. "Oh, no. No, indeed. You mustn't think that. I wouldn't—"

"You wouldn't?" Eliza could not have hidden her astonishment if she'd tried.

"Oh, no, of course not. I simply explained to Mr.

Slaughter that my father had expressly forbidden me to speak to him and that I'd be grateful if he'd ride on. And he did."

"He just rode off? That's all?"

"Certainly. You must remember he was once a gentleman."

Eliza let that pass. "But I had understood that you and he used to be—well, quite close."

"That was before I knew his true character."

"Are you quite certain that you know it now? What if he's not guilty?"

Lady Juliet was now looking at Eliza as though her mentality were suspect. "Of course he's guilty. I'm amazed that you don't know it. But then, I think your aunt said you've spent no time in London. I can assure you that the ton talked of little else. The scandal was not only the *on-dit* of the season, it eclipsed anything that had been heard of in years. And Papa says my own name was sure to have been dragged through the mire because of it. I must tell you, Miss Osborne, it was all more than I could countenance. Why, I actually stayed away from Lady Jersey's rout on the strength of it."

If she had expected a cluck of sympathy from Miss Osborne after this revelation, Lady Juliet was disappointed. Instead, Eliza probed a bit deeper. "But just suppose evidence was uncovered that would prove his innocence?"

"But how could that be? It was an open-and-shut case. The jewels were found in his coat pocket."

"But—" The defense was cut short by the entrance of the gentlemen. Jervis Wenham was making a beeline in their direction. Eliza noted that his limp lessened considerably under the goddess's welcoming smile.

After a civil exchange with Mr. Wenham, which he somehow managed without ever looking at her, Eliza was on the point of excusing herself when Lady Cheselden bore down upon them. "There's to be cards, Charlotte says. You and I, Miss Osborne, will take on these two at whist."

"Oh, but there are too many of us," Eliza, who could count to fourteen as well as anyone, quickly observed. "I shall be only too glad to sit out and let someone else take my place."

"Oh, do play, please, Miss Osborne," Lady Juliet pleaded. She was obviously intimidated by the prospect of cards with Lady Cheselden and needed moral support.

"Yes, do join us."

Eliza did not delude herself. She realized that Jervis's earnest invitation was on Lady Juliet's behalf.

"It's all been settled." Lady Cheselden, with a thump of her stick, brought the discussion to a close. "Wenham and the vicar aren't playing. That leaves three tables. Come on."

As they trailed her ladyship to the other side of the enormous room, where the servants were arranging tables and setting out the cards, Eliza felt a stab of envy for her uncle and his lordship. They were retreating toward the latter's study, no doubt to blow a cloud and have a comfortable coze.

She almost got a reprieve. Just as Jervis had begun to shuffle the cards, Lady Wenham bore down upon them. "Oh, Miss Osborne, you're to play at Sir Joshua's table. Miss Hurst will partner Mama."

Eliza rose obediently, but Lady Cheselden waved her back down with an imperious gesture. "No, I don't wish to play with Hurst. She's got no more card sense than a flea."

Lady Wenham looked annoyed but did not see fit to argue the point. It was not worth a scene, evidently, to keep Eliza from her son's table.

Eliza smiled to herself. If her ladyship really believed she posed any kind of threat to her careful matchmaking, well, it was flattering, but a bunch of moonshine. It became more and more obvious throughout the evening that Jervis had eyes for no one else but the fair Juliet.

And at first Eliza believed that his distraction accounted for her and her partner's winning streak. She had little doubt that he could be an astute player under other circumstances, for no matter what else she might think of him, she did not doubt his intelligence. True, Lady Juliet was a liability. Though she concentrated painfully on her cards, she constantly blundered into the traps that Lady Cheselden set for her, much to the old crone's cackled delight. But it gradually became apparent that Eliza could not contribute their success either to Jervis's distraction or to Lady Juliet's ineptitude. The fact was, Lady Cheselden was a cheat.

And not a particularly subtle one at that. For if Mr. Wenham had not been so intent on gazing at his partner, he might have seen his grandmother looking at his hand. And even though Eliza tried to ignore the signals the old lady sent her, surely the opposition would soon awaken to what was going on? But when, for a third time, her ladyship played a card from a suit she'd formerly claimed to be out of, Eliza decided this was the outside of enough. She was just opening her mouth to say so when a sharp kick to the shin stopped her. But when she turned to ring a peal over Mr. Wenham for this unprovoked attack, he gave his head a warning shake, his eyes glinting with amusement.

Why, he knew that his grandmother cheated and didn't wish the old horror to be called on it. It was simply an accepted part of the game. Come to think on it, that, no doubt, was why Lady Wenham had wanted Miss Hurst to partner her, to keep Lady Cheselden's peccadilloes in the family, as it were. How lowering. Just when she'd concluded that at least one person considered her a worthy rival of the fair Juliet.

"I need to speak to you," she managed to whisper to Jervis while Lady Cheselden was lecturing Lady Juliet on just how she should have played the previous hand. The other was listening intently like an obedient schoolroom pupil.

Mr. Wenham, looking less than delighted at the prospect, nodded. Then later on, when the tea board was carried in, he followed her across the room. She was pretending to examine the music on the pianoforte. Eliza came directly to the point. "Did you know that your scheme to leave Lady Juliet and Mr. Slaughter together didn't work? She wouldn't talk to him."

"Yes, I do know. She told me."

"Well." She glared accusingly. "Don't you think you should do something about it?"

"What can I do?" He glared back. "Her papa—"

"Oh, bother her papa! You certainly could let her know that you believe he's innocent."

"But I can't tell her that. Actually, I'm not sure what I believe."

"Oh, yes, you are," she hissed. "You know you don't think he did it, and you've no right—"

"Very well, then." He cut off the whispered tirade. "Have it your way. I'll try again. I'll drive Lady Juliet out to the abbey ruins tomorrow. You can tell Garrick to be there. After that, it's up to him."

"Jervis, m'dear." Lady Wenham was bearing down upon them. Her artificial smile was fixed in place, but the plumes in her hair fairly quivered with annoyance. "Should you not be taking tea to Lady Juliet? I fear that your grandmama is becoming tedious with her reminiscing. I know her ladyship longs for rescue. And I'm sure Miss Osborne will excuse you." With another cool smile in Eliza's direction, she whisked her son away.

Well, at least that bit of business was gratifying. Eliza hid an impish smile behind her fan. Lady Wenham did consider her a threat to her matrimonial scheming after all.

Chapter
Twelve

"**S**top that this instant!" *Eliza shrieked while she* picked up a bucket of water beside the horse trough and dashed it over the two combatants. She had gone in search of Mr. Slaughter and, not finding him in his cottage, had followed the sound of battle to the stable. There, he and a muscular young man, both stripped to the waist, were standing toe to toe pummeling one another. "Fighting like two schoolboys!" she yelled as the gasping, drenched combatants sprang apart. "Have you lost your minds?"

"Not entirely," Mr. Slaughter sputtered as he wiped his streaming face, "but much more association with you, Miss Osborne, and I vow I will. This, Jim, in case you're wondering, is the vicar's niece. And Jim is my groom, not my deadly enemy. And we were not fighting—that is, not in the way you mean. We were practicing for a mill."

"A mill?"

"Boxing match. Thank you, Jim. It would appear we're through for the day." He walked over and retrieved two shirts from the ground and tossed one toward the groom, who caught it and disappeared into the stable.

"You wished to see me?" The inquiry was muffled as Mr. Slaughter pulled his shirt over his head.

But Eliza was not so easily diverted. "What do you mean you're practicing for a mill?"

"I just told you. A boxing match. Fisticuffs."

"You mean you actually intend to fight?"

"That's why I'm practicing."

"But where? And why?"

"Where? In Brighton. Why? Because I happen to be rather good at it and the prize money's handsome. But enough of this. You tell me why you're seeking out my disreputable company."

"I wish you to take me to see the abbey ruins."

"Why?"

"Because I've been told it's one of the local sights that one should see."

"Well, I realize we're rather hard put to provide entertainment for our tourists, but we can surely do better than that crumbling pile of stones."

"But I particularly wish to see it."

"Suit yourself. But if you can come here without an escort, you can certainly go there. I'll direct you."

"Oh, bother. You are so exasperating. The thing is, you have to come."

"Why?"

"Because I've arranged for Lady Juliet to be there."

His face was suddenly drained of all expression, as revealing as a mask. "You really should learn to stay out of other people's affairs, Miss Osborne," he said coolly. "Lady Juliet does not wish to speak to me. Ever. She made that quite clear at our last meeting."

"That's when she believed you were guilty."

"And that's all changed? I hardly think so."

"Well, let's just say she's prepared to be open-minded." At least Eliza hoped that was true. It would be if Jervis Wenham had had the integrity to lay the groundwork properly.

It took a great deal more persuasion, a testimonial to just how deeply the beauty had hurt him, she surmised, before Eliza at last persuaded Mr. Slaughter to accompany her. She waited impatiently while he went to change his clothes. "Finally," she said when he appeared down the pathway that led from the cottage to the stable. But she had to concede that he'd made good use of his time. He was wearing a cinnamon-colored riding coat and white buckskins. His cravat was modest but impeccable. His boots gleamed with blacking. His hair was carefully arranged under the low-crowned beaver. She wished he'd gone to such lengths for her benefit.

"Oh, do hurry," she protested later as they trudged cross-country toward their destination. "Every other time I've walked anywhere with you I've practically had to run to keep up. Now a snail would put you to shame."

"Oh, are you afraid that the newly converted Lady Juliet won't wait?" His voice was mocking. "And here I thought she deeply desired this meeting."

Eliza studied his face thoughtfully. "She really did put your nose out of joint, didn't she?"

"Let's just say that it's not an especially uplifting experience to have the lady you fancied yourself in love with treat you like a particularly loathsome type of vermin."

"I collect you exaggerate. But at any rate you must remember that Lady Juliet has led a sheltered life. And she appears to be very much under her parents' thumbs. I'm sure that the mere idea of going against her father's wishes is most unsettling."

"Unlike some young women of my acquaintance."

She reddened. "Comparisons really are odious, you know. As well as unnecessary. It's Lady Juliet's sensibilities that are in question, not mine."

"Oh, well, then. Thank you for setting me straight on that point. There're your ruins. Think it's worth the hike?"

As to that, Eliza couldn't say. She took little interest in the crumbling remnants of stone walls and towers that crowned the rise before them. Her eyes were too busy scanning the landscape for a curricle. "Oh, blast!" she said, almost beneath her breath.

"Looks like a fool's errand," he jeered. "Shall we go home now?"

"Of course not. They'll be here. Besides, I want to see the abbey."

But she was seething as she tramped through the grassy remnants of what had once been the abbey chapel. Where was Jervis Wenham, anyhow? It was obvious that he was falling under Lady Juliet's spell. He must have had second thoughts about giving his rival a chance to plead his case. Perhaps she shouldn't blame him, but she did. Fair was fair.

Just when she'd abandoned hope entirely and was ready to give in to her escort's repeated demands to leave, Eliza heard the sound of a carriage coming fast. She climbed precariously on a stone wall and shielded her eyes with her hands. "Oh, good. There he is." She watched the curricle leave the distant road and head cross-country toward them.

"He'll be lucky if he doesn't upset her" was Garrick's only comment.

As the rig drew near, two things became apparent. First, Lady Juliet, wearing a blue velvet bonnet and carriage dress the exact same shade of her eyes, had never looked more fetching; and second, she had not had the slightest inkling she would see Mr. Slaughter. She looked, in point of fact, appalled.

Her voice was much too low for whatever she was saying to be overheard, but Eliza had little doubt that she was instructing Mr. Wenham to drive on by. Judging from the grim set of his face as he rose slowly to his feet, Garrick Slaughter was of the same opinion.

"Why, hullo. Didn't expect to find anyone else actually wishing to see this pile of rocks."

Jervis's greeting could have done with a bit more rehearsal, Eliza thought. It certainly rang false. But at least he'd managed to make clear what she'd suspected: He had not pleaded Garrick's case and persuaded Lady Juliet to meet with him.

Jervis climbed awkwardly from the curricle, but her ladyship rejected the hand he offered to help her down. "Oh, I am sorry, Jervis, but it seems much too hot for exploring, don't you think?" To emphasize the point she picked up the ruffled blue sunshade lying on the seat beside her and opened it.

"Oh, but it would be a pity not to see the ruins," Jervis protested.

His half brother had heard enough. "It's quite all right, Lady Juliet. You may stay. Miss Osborne and I were just leaving."

"Oh, but I didn't mean . . ." As she gazed at Mr. Slaughter, Lady Juliet looked quite distressed, a condition that did not mar her beauty one whit, Eliza noticed.

"Of course you did. But never mind. Come on, Miss Osborne."

Eliza opened her mouth to protest, then had a better notion. She obediently jumped down from the wall she stood on, turned an ankle, and landed with a thud on her behind.

"Oh, my heavens! Are you all right?" her ladyship called out anxiously, while both gentlemen regarded Eliza with similar looks of detachment.

"N-no, I don't really think so. I've twisted my ankle, I'm afraid." Her suffering was unfeigned, though the ankle she was rubbing vigorously was not the seat of her discomfort. There was more verisimilitude than she'd intended in her fall.

"Oh, I say, do you think you can walk?" Mr. Wenham had been a bit slow to pick up his cue, but now he threw himself wholeheartedly into the performance.

"It will amaze me if she can," Mr. Slaughter remarked dryly as he helped Eliza to her feet.

"Ouch!" Miss Osborne's ejaculation was caused not so much from trying to place her weight upon her foot as from the excessive pressure on her arm.

She tried a few tentative steps and was relieved to find she'd not done herself too much damage. "Oh, dear." She winced, trying to appear brave. "I do fear I've sprained it." She sank piteously back down upon the ground and looked at Jervis expectantly.

This time there was no groping for his lines. "I'd best drive you straight off to the doctor," he declared. "Lady Juliet, you won't mind waiting here a bit, will you? There's really not enough room for the three of us. I shan't be long."

"Oh, but . . ." The lady's distress increased.

"Don't concern yourself. I'm sure that after she rests a bit, Miss Osborne will be quite able to walk home," said Mr. Slaughter.

"That's easy for you to say." The patient in question glared at Mr. Slaughter.

"If the worst comes to worst, I can always carry you," he informed her sweetly.

"Well, really, if Lady Juliet does not object, I'd much prefer to be driven."

"Then allow me to do so. Jervis, will you trust me with your rig?"

"You know that I can't walk any distance on my bad foot, Garrick."

"You and Miss Osborne really are a pair. It's hard to decide who's more pathetic."

"My, what a to-do everyone is making." Eliza rose clumsily to her feet. "Lady Juliet, if you're afraid to be left alone with Mr. Slaughter, may I remind you that it was theft he was accused of, not an ax murder."

"Really, Miss Osborne," the beauty shot back with more spirit than Eliza had thought her capable of, "that's a horrid thing to say. I am not afraid of Mr. Slaughter. It's simply that I promised Mama, but under the circumstances ..." She shrugged prettily and climbed down from the carriage.

"I can always leave," Mr. Slaughter observed.

"Don't be ridiculous, Garrick. I'll not stay here alone." She looked around as though the ruins might be haunted. "Pray don't be long, Jervis. You know how Mama frets."

"I doubt that 'Mama' will fret as long as she thinks her daughter's with you," Eliza observed *sotto voce* after she'd been helped into the rig and Jervis had sprung his horses.

"You really are rather shrewish, you know," he retorted as they went racing down the hill.

"I'm sorry. I realize it's unbecoming in a female. But, for heaven's sake, slow down. We're out of sight now and the point of this charade was to give those two some time together, if you remember."

"I'm not likely to forget it." His voice was grim as he pulled back on the reins.

They rode in silence for a bit; Mr. Wenham sulked while Miss Osborne thought. "Did you know there's to be a mill in Brighton?" she asked abruptly.

"Why, no." He perked up. "Are you sure? Who told you?"

"Your bro—Mr. Slaughter, I mean to say."

"Oh, come now. Isn't it a bit late for you to act so missish? God knows you weren't shy before about discussing our relationship. But forget all that. How did my *brother* come to hear of the mill?"

"He's fighting in it."

"You're bamming."

"Of course I'm not. I saw him practicing. He's supposed to fight somebody called the 'Savage' something or other."

"Savage Stenhouse?" Jervis turned rather pale.

"Why, yes, I think so. In fact, I'm quite sure of it now." She looked at Jervis in alarm. "Is that bad?"

"Bad? He'll kill him."

"I collect you mean that the Savage Whoever will kill your brother and not vice versa."

"Of course that's what I mean, you pea-goose."

"Well, how should I know? When I asked Mr. Slaughter why he was planning to do such a bird-witted thing, he said that he was quite good at boxing."

"Well, he is in the normal way of things. That is, among gentlemen he's said to be quite handy with his fives. He and his set strip with Jackson, actually."

"Whatever that should mean."

"Surely you know that Gentleman Jackson was the champion of England. Well, he has this place in Bond Street where members of the fancy go to work out. And Garrick, so they tell me, was his star pupil. But that don't mean he can stand up against the Savage. My God, Eliza, the man's bigger than the bull that chased you up the tree, and ten times as mean."

"Oh." Eliza was paler now than he was. "Will you take me there?"

"To see the mill?" He was horrified. "Of course not. Ladies don't attend prizefights."

"Well, they go to fairs, don't they? And it shouldn't present much difficulty to ease from the exhibits over to where the fight is taking place."

"No!" Mr. Wenham's face set stubbornly as they turned into the village street. "I couldn't take you there even if I wished and, believe me, I do not— Oh, my God!" He broke off in consternation and tugged back on the reins as he spied his grandmother stalking down the vicarage walkway, leaning heavily on her coachman's arm. The inquisitive black eyes were peering their way.

"Drive on by," Eliza hissed while averting her head so that the brim of her poke bonnet would shield her face from sight. "Perhaps she'll think I'm Lady Juliet."

"Huh!" But he obediently flicked the reins and they passed the vicarage gateway in a cloud of dust.

"You can pull up now and I'll walk back," Eliza said when they were out of sight. "I really think we fooled her, don't you, Mr. Wenham?"

"No, I don't," was the curt reply. "My grandmother may be a bit dotty, but she ain't that daft. There's no way she could mistake you for Lady Juliet."

"Well, thank you very much," Eliza said through gritted teeth as she jumped down unaided.

"Best watch that ankle!" he spat back with equal venom.

Her retort was drowned out by the loud crack of his driving whip.

Chapter Thirteen

It came as no great surprise the next morning when Eliza received a summons to the Hall. The message, delivered by a footman wearing the Wenham livery, was that Lady Cheselden wished her to take up *Humphry Clinker* where she'd left off. But Eliza thought it far more likely that Jervis was right, they hadn't fooled her ladyship one little bit.

She toyed with the idea of begging off. But it would only do her uncle a disservice to upset his patron's mama-in-law. She'd best go and let the old behemoth have her say.

It seemed to her that the starchy butler looked even more disapproving than usual when he opened the door in answer to her knock. His greeting did nothing to dispel that impression. "Lady Wenham would like a word with you, miss, before you go to read to Lady Cheselden. She's waiting in the library."

It did seem unfair, Eliza thought irrelevantly as the butler bowed her into Lady Wenham's presence, that she was always either being whisked through Warleigh Hall without a moment's pause to appreciate its grandeur or else she was too distracted when the opportunity arose to see it properly. Consider this room, for instance, with its Etruscan reliefs, its plasterwork and porphyry columns, its row upon row of tempting volumes that invited one to browse. It all simply clamored for rapt attention. But the best she could manage was a mere glance. The formidable woman seated at the pedestal library table was far too compelling.

"Pray take a seat, Miss Osborne."

Eliza sat in the indicated spoon-backed chair, thinking that this was how an upstairs maid must feel when called upon the carpet for failing to dust the wardrobe top. Still, though, the maid would not be asked to sit.

Her ladyship was not one for mincing words. "My mother informs me that you were out riding with my son yesterday, Miss Osborne."

"Why, no, m'lady. That is to say, yes, I did in fact ride with him, of course. But we were not 'out riding' in the sense you seem to mean it."

"If you are trying to draw some distinction, Miss Osborne, I quite fail to follow it."

Eliza thought of her uncle and stopped just short of saying that she owed her ladyship no explanation. Instead, she replied civilly, "I simply mean that I had gone to see the abbey ruins and while there I turned my ankle. Your son and Lady Juliet happened along and he kindly offered to take me home. That is all there was to that."

"Is it, indeed, Miss Osborne?" Lady Wenham's fine, dark eyebrows almost met her snow-white cap. "It appears to me there must be a great deal more to it than that. In the first place, why were you at such pains to avoid Lady Cheselden?"

"Perhaps you should ask your son that question since he was driving." This time, Eliza could not quite keep her temper in check. "It could be he felt that much ado would be made over nothing."

Lady Wenham let that pass. "But what seems even more odd, Miss Osborne, is the miraculous recovery you appear to have made. You did say Jervis deserted his houseguest—whose welfare was his first responsibility—because you had sprained your ankle and were quite unable to walk. And yet today you walk with no apparent difficulty. I did not detect even a trace of a limp when you came into this room."

Botheration! How could she have been so bird-witted? "It did not prove as serious as it first appeared." This sounded a great deal more lame than her condition. Still, it was the best she could manage.

"I'm sure that it did not. Indeed I suggest to you, Miss Osborne, that there was never anything wrong with your ankle. Twisting it was merely a ploy, a device for getting my son alone with you."

Lady Wenham seemed to be waiting for a rebuttal, but since the accusation was near enough the truth, Eliza thought it best simply to say nothing.

"Well, at least I see you haven't the gall to deny it. I must point out, Miss Osborne, that my son, due to his—infirmity—has led a rather restricted life. A less . . . unworldly gentleman would have seen right through your subterfuge."

"Are you saying that Mr. Wenham is a flat?" Ever since she'd learned the term from Garrick Slaughter, Eliza had been trying to work it into a conversation. Something now told her that this had not been the proper time. Two angry spots burned in Lady Wenham's cheeks.

"I am saying no such thing. I'm simply pointing out that while any gentleman is prone to be easy prey for females of a certain stamp, Jervis's limited experience makes him even more susceptible than most. And I am warning you, Miss Osborne, to stop casting out your lures."

But Eliza was on her feet now, fighting down the desire to fling the open inkpot at her ladyship. Her voice shook with anger, but that did not detract from her haughty bearing. "Indeed you shall not warn me of anything, Lady Wenham, for I refuse to sit here and be insulted further. If you wish to create a scene over the fact that your son did an act of kindness, I suppose that is your privilege. But only as long as you read the 'riot act' to your mollycoddled offspring and not to me."

And with that speech, which left her ladyship gasping, Eliza swept from the room. Her dramatic exit was only slightly marred by the fact that in her blind rage she blundered into a candle screen and sent it reeling.

Her inclination, once she reached the hall, was to race for the door and not stop till she reached the sanctuary of the vicarage. But pride and the Wenham butler nipped the impulse in the bud. "Lady Cheselden is waiting, miss." The majordomo's face was blank, impassive. But for all that, Eliza was willing to wager he'd had his ear plastered against the keyhole.

She was still shaking with rage when he opened the door to Lady Cheselden's apartments. "Come in, come in," the old lady called out impatiently. The black eyes studied Eliza gleefully as she took the indicated chair on the opposite side of the tea table. "Well, now, miss. Out with it. What's put you into such a taking?"

"Your daughter has just referred to me as a 'female of a certain stamp.'"

"Did she now?" The old woman cackled. "Well, I'm not surprised a bit by it, I can tell you. For Charlotte has that particular maggot on the brain. Even after all these years she's still jealous of Lord

Wenham's lightskirt. She's bound and determined to marry Jervis off before he gets entangled with that sort."

"And she puts me in that category?" Eliza's temper went on the boil again.

"Oh, do come down off your high bough. I doubt she goes that far in her thinking, but she certainly doesn't consider you an eligible match for her only son. Why, I told you myself, he's way above your touch. What's more, Charlotte's determined that Jervis's marriage will be a love match. No rival's going to interfere with him falling head over heels with the right girl if she can help it."

It was Eliza's unexpressed opinion that Jervis's mother need not worry. He was well and truly smitten, if she was any judge. But she wasn't going to give his grandmother her reassurance. They sat in silence as a maid carried in a refreshment tray.

The moment the door closed, her ladyship reopened the subject. "Charlotte's problem, you see, is that she's always believed Wenham was in love with his doxy. That she was the love of his life, in fact. And it's probably true," the old lady editorialized through a mouthful of seedcake, "for the girl died, don't you see, before he'd time to tire of her and pension her off the way any normal gentleman would have done. That's why he had his brat fetched here to be brought up under his nose. And every time he looked at the boy, he'd remember his whore."

Perhaps it was because she thought so little of her ladyship's terminology that Eliza snapped back, "Well, I don't see why he'd do that since Mr. Slaughter looks exactly like *him*."

"Don't be pert. I'm looking at the thing from Charlotte's point of view. *She* certainly thought of the whore every time she saw the lad.

"And do you know what the biggest joke in the whole business was? Everyone thought Charlotte

103

was beyond childbearing when she married Wenham. Her father and I had given up on her, and that's God's truth. She seemed doomed to stay an old maid."

"I don't see why. She's still a handsome woman, and I should think she was something of a beauty in her youth," Eliza said.

"Of course she was. All the women in our family have been for generations. Oh, she couldn't hold a candle to what I once was, though. Nor did the gentlemen flock around her the way they courted me. She was pretty enough, you see, but she lacked that certain something that gentlemen can sense about a female. Well, I had it by the bucketful myself, as my late husband, as well as a few others, could have testified." She cackled wickedly.

With a twinge of conscience as she once more recalled her aunt's strictures against gossiping, Eliza tried to steer the old lady back on course. "It still seems odd that Lady Wenham waited so late to marry. For even if she didn't have your way with the other sex, there was still the matter of her fortune."

"Actually, Charlotte was betrothed right after her come-out. But her fiancé died of a pox. And, well, after that no one ever seemed to suit her until Wenham came along. And I'll tell you this, miss, my daughter may appear a cold fish, but she tumbled arsy-varsy for his lordship, no mistake."

Eliza could well believe it. As far as she was concerned, all the Wenham men should be posted with DANGER! KEEP OUT! signs. Even churlish Jervis with his limp was a decided threat.

"I don't think it concerned Charlotte at all that Wenham was after her fortune," Lady Cheselden was droning on. "That's to be expected in our class. But what had eaten at her for all these years is that he may have chosen her because he, too, believed she was too old to have any children and that eventually he could make his bastard his heir.

"I'll vow Charlotte conceived from sheer determination. She'd had two miscarriages before Jervis, don't you know. And the doctor warned her against trying for another child. But there was no way she was going to let Wenham leave her bed." Again her ladyship paused for a wicked chuckle, but then she sobered. "Well, when Jervis was finally born he was marred, don't you see. It nearly killed my Charlotte, let me tell you."

"It's too bad, of course. But it does seem to me that all of you make far too much of what is, after all, a fairly minor affliction. Mr. Wenham would have been the better, I'd think, for being treated normally." Eliza waited for the inevitable explosion.

Instead, she received a withering glare. "You needn't take that preachy tone with me, Miss Know-It-All. For you miss the point entirely. I doubt Charlotte would have made a Cheltenham tragedy out of a clubfoot normally. But how else could she feel with that bastard growing up right under their noses where her husband couldn't help but make comparisons? The trollop's son was perfect, don't you see. Hers was flawed. She couldn't deal with that."

"But that's absurd. True, Mr. Wenham has a limp, but he's handsome and extremely intelligent—and he rides like a cavalryman. He's a nonesuch whip. I don't believe for a moment that Lord Wenham could find him a disappointment. That's all in Lady Wenham's mind."

"Of course it is." The old lady surprised her by agreeing. "But the true or false of the thing is of no consequence. As you'd know if you were older and had some experience of the world. It's what a person gets in her mind and lets stick there that makes the difference. That's the *real* truth, young miss."

Eliza mulled those words over as she walked home, after first putting Lady Cheselden to sleep with one more chapter of *Humphry Clinker*. There was no doubt in her mind that Lady Wenham was completely irrational where her son was concerned. The fact she'd created a scene over the "crime" of a curricle ride testified to that. And her own mother believed that her jealousy of her husband's by-blow passed all normal bounds. But could she have been jealous enough to send that son to prison?

It was hard for Eliza to imagine such wickedness. Still, she was now convinced that it was Lady Wenham whom Garrick Slaughter suspected of putting the jewels in his pocket. And she'd bet a monkey that Jervis Wenham suspected his mother as well.

Oh, Lady Wenham was the logical suspect, no doubt about it. But even if she was the guilty party, how could one ever prove it? Eliza thought of little else for the remainder of the day but quite despaired of ever finding a solution to her quandary.

She was still hatching up preposterous schemes for tricking Lady Wenham into a confession when she was interrupted by a knock on her chamber door at five o'clock that evening. Betty, Mrs. Tomkins's maid-of-all-work, poked her head in to announce that a gentleman wished a word with her. "It's Mr. Wenham, not that other one," she added as Eliza slid eagerly off her bed.

"What other one?" Miss Osborne inquired frostily. Betty's only answer was a knowing smile over her shoulder. She left Eliza wondering how it was that servants always seemed to know everything about their lives.

Upon her entrance Mr. Wenham stopped his pacing back and forth in the small withdrawing room. His face was thunderous. "I'm here to say I'll take you to the . . . fair tomorrow if you still wish to go there," he announced abruptly.

Eliza was careful to close the door behind her before she answered. "Oh, yes, I definitely wish it. But what changed your mind?"

"Mama!" he spat, resuming his rapid striding. "I understand she raked you over the coals for driving with me. I'll not have her interfering in my life as if I were still in leading strings."

"Well, I can certainly understand your attitude," Eliza said diplomatically, "but yet I don't like to think of you getting into her black books on my account. What I mean to say is, I see no need for your defiance. Can't you just pick me up someplace where the whole world won't see us and carry the news back to her? And what about Lady Juliet? Do you think she might wish to come along?"

"Lady Juliet go to a mill? You must be funning."

"Not at all. It would depend entirely on how concerned she is about Mr. Slaughter being battered to a pulp."

"Oh, she'd be concerned all right if she knew about it. But that don't mean she'd want to see it happen."

"Would you please stop pacing? You're making me positively giddy. And pray sit down and tell me what happened yesterday."

He plummeted into a wing chair at the peril of its structure and she sat opposite him. "You know damn well what happened," he growled. "By the time I got back to the ruins Lady Juliet had spent forty-five minutes alone with Garrick. He's the very devil with the ladies, you know."

Well, she did and she didn't. Her first impression had been formed of the odoriferous, ragged, bearded convict, not of the Bond Street beau. Still, that had been unsettling enough.

"But what actually happened when you got back?"

"What do you think happened? They were waiting where we left them. Garrick handed her into the curricle, said good-bye, and I drove off with her."

"Don't be so caper-witted. You know perfectly well what I mean. How did they seem?"

"I've told you all I know."

"You most certainly have not. You're bound to have noticed whether they were happy or sad. Angry or indifferent. Oh, botheration! Don't be so obtuse. Had they or had they not made up their differences?"

"How the hell would I know? They didn't spring apart from a passionate embrace as I drove up, if that's what you mean."

"Well, surely you must have asked Lady Juliet what happened."

"Of course I didn't. What do you take me for? Besides, she wasn't supposed to know that you'd hatched all this up in order to throw Garrick at her head, now, was she? All she seemed to want to talk about was you and your curst ankle. I think the poor widgeon believes you'll be crippled for life, like me."

Eliza was imprudent enough to giggle then, which earned her another glare. She deemed it time to change the subject. "When shall we leave tomorrow?"

"Ten, I'd think. The fight's at noon and though it's only an hour's drive in the normal way of things, there's bound to be a lot of traffic."

"Why don't we go at nine then and see some of the fair?"

"Won't do. Mama and Lady Juliet and Lady Greenwood are spending the day at Hale House. Best wait till they leave."

"Oh, very well then." So he wasn't as rebellious as he'd first appeared.

They settled on a meeting place and she walked

with him to his carriage. "So you really think we went through that whole business yesterday for nothing?" Eliza grimaced as she recalled her unpleasant interview with Lady Wenham.

"Of course I don't think that!" he snapped. "Didn't I just say that Garrick and Juliet spent three-quarters of an hour together? Well, use your head for once."

And with that dampening instruction he left Eliza standing there in a cloud of dust obediently thinking of the Beauty and the Devil-with-the-Ladies alone together in the romantic ruins.

Chapter Fourteen

In spite of his predictions, even Mr. Wenham was not prepared for the congestion of carriages, carts, and wagons that clogged the outskirts of Brighton. Their curricle crept along at a snail's pace that was absolutely maddening to the impatient passengers. And as Eliza covered her nose with a handkerchief in order to filter out some of the thick clouds of dust they were breathing, she could not help envying those fortunates in the enclosed coaches and said so.

"You did insist on coming," her escort snapped. "So spare me your complaints."

"I am not complaining. I merely pointed out that if we had known, we might have chosen some other equipage, that's all."

"Well," he grudgingly admitted, "if I'd been thinking properly, I should have hidden you away. You won't catch any other females going to a mill."

"Oh, for heaven's sake, don't start that again."
She sighed as some unseen complication ahead
ground their snail's pace to a complete halt. "As
far as anyone can tell, we're merely going to the
fair. Or to gawk at the pavilion. Or to—"

"Oh, I say, young sir!" a genial voice rang out
from a gig pulled up beside them. "Going to the
mill, then, are you?" A dandyish fellow was sizing
Jervis up. "Care for a little flutter? I've five pounds
that say the Savage'll slaughter Slaughter in the
second round." The sporting man laughed uproari-
ously at his play on words.

"You won't get no takers for that one, guv,"
someone in a pony cart behind them hooted. "Not
unless you give 'em odds you won't."

"Pay 'em no mind." This voice spoke confidentially and came from a pedestrian who was picking
his way among the stalled vehicles to reach the
other side of the road, which appeared a bit more
conducive to foot travel. He was a small man of
early middle age. His clothes aped those of a gentleman but had obviously never been in the vicinity
of Bond Street. They atoned for their ill fit by flash-
iness. The bright green of his coat and the yellow
of his pantaloons were far too vivid to be dulled by
their layer of dust. This luminous quality was en-
hanced by the bogus diamond on his watch fob,
which reflected the feeble rays of the sun through
clouds like the looking glass it had been destined
for. His smile was just as sparkling when he flashed
it while doffing a sweat-stained beaver. "Take a tip
from me, young gentleman." He kept his voice low
and looked surreptitiously all around him.
"Wouldn't want the word to spread and spoil the
odds, but if you want a piece of advice, put your
blunt on Mr. Slaughter. 'Appen to know 'im personally, I do, and believe me, he'll do for the Savage."

"Oh, do you really think so?" Eliza's eyes glowed

while Jervis frowned at her for encouraging such raffish familiarity.

"Couldn't be more sure of anything in this uncertain world." The pedestrian broke his journey to come stand beside their rig. "Sold all me worldly goods, I 'ave, and plan to punt the lot. That's 'ow confident I am in Mr. Slaughter."

"I believe you mentioned that you know him," Eliza was saying when the vehicle just ahead started to move once more and Jervis clucked at his bays. "Oh, dear, we're off again. I say, wouldn't you like to ride behind on the tiger's perch?"

"Don't be daft. He'll make much better time on foot." Jervis shot her a darkling glance, which both she and the pedestrian ignored.

"Why, thank'ee, miss." The little man climbed gratefully up behind them and grasped the straps. "It's nip and tuck whether me boot soles will make it the rest of the way. And I was unwillin', don't you see, to spring for coach fare. I wished to keep me capital intact for wagering."

"How is it that you come to know Mr. Slaughter?" Eliza inquired politely as she half turned on the seat to facilitate conversation.

"How do you think?" Jervis growled, ostensibly for her ears alone, but the comment was picked up by their passenger.

He looked rather taken aback, but only momentarily. "A regular knowing 'un you are for a fact, sir. Oh, 'e's 'it it square on the nailhead, miss. I 'ad the 'onor of sharing a Newgate bed with Mr. Slaughter. Along of twenty-two other misfortunates. No need to be shifting your reticule, though. The crime I was wrongfully convicted of 'ad nothing to do with pickpocketing."

"What did it have to do with?" Mr. Wenham asked bluntly.

"A domestic altercation, you might say. I found a stranger occupying me bed alongside of me wife, you see. And it's 'ard to say which of us was the most surprised. But in the long run 'e was the most inconvenienced."

There was a pregnant pause while Miss Osborne and Mr. Wenham digested this revelation.

"Er, speaking of beds." Miss Osborne struggled to regain her composure. "Surely you were funning just now when you said that Mr. Slaughter shared a bed with all those people."

"I can assure you, miss, prison beds is no joking matter. 'Beds' is a misleading term, you see, miss. What we're h'actually talking about 'ere is a section of wooden flooring that's inclined a bit, with a beam crossing the top of it for a pillow. They give every prisoner a pair of rugs to sleep on, but good luck keepin' 'em. There's always somebody as gets greedy and wants a bit more padding for 'isself."

"How horrible." Eliza shuddered.

"Ah, well, you can get used to anything," the man remarked philosophically. "The sleeping arrangements was the best of it, h'actually. They'd worked it out to a fair science, don't you see, and 'ad concluded that a common-sized man only needs nineteen inches of space to turn in. But most of the time the wards was so crowded with all those poor devils waitin' to be shifted to the hulks that there wasn't even walking space. Then the barracks beds was luxury, I'll tell you. And you 'ad to be something out of the ordinary to get and 'old one."

There was a profound silence while the young lady and gentleman digested this insider information. Their guest seemed concerned that he'd cast a pall upon their morning and cheerfully strove to divert their thoughts. "Come to think on it, I've not introduced meself proper-like, now, 'ave I? Crake's me name. Barnaby Crake." He paused expectantly.

"I'm Miss Osborne." Eliza stepped into the breach when Jervis, who was looking decidedly ill, failed to do the proper. "And this is Mr. Wenham."

"Pleased to make your acquaintance, I'm sure."

"I don't see what the devil my—Mr. Slaughter—was doing in a place like that." Jervis was not diverted.

"Well, they said as 'ow 'e'd nicked some jewelry, though I for one am inclined to doubt it."

"No, no." Jervis shook his head impatiently. "That's not what I mean. The thing is, I was given to understand that it was possible to secure fairly decent accommodations in prison if you had the blunt. And Mr. Slaughter was no pauper."

"That's true, you can, sir. But the way of it was, you see, Mr. Slaughter got put in with the common herd of us before the machinery could be put in motion to get 'im transferred. And, well, after that one night's experience, 'e decided 'e could put his blunt to better use. I tell you, one night in Newgate is an education that the likes of you young toffs wouldn't dream of at your Etons and your Harrows."

"I never went to Eton or to Harrow," Jervis said impatiently. "But never mind all that. Just tell us what happened to Mr. Slaughter." The traffic was moving at a slow but steady pace, and a signpost indicated they were only three miles from Brighton.

"Well, I don't know as 'ow the story's fit for a lady's ears, sir."

"Don't worry about me," Eliza prodded. "Just tell us what happened that first night."

"Well, if you insist. The thing was, you see, Mr. Slaughter created something of a stir when he came amongst us, seeing as 'ow 'e was a swell and ripe for the pluckin' as it were. So 'e was immediately put on trial."

"On trial! Whatever do you mean? He'd already been tried before he was imprisoned."

"That was on the outside, miss. Every prison 'as its own judicial system, so to speak."

114

"But what in God's name was he tried for?" Jervis asked.

"Now you mention it, I don't rightly recall. Could've been for anything—treading on somebody's toe or jostling agin' somebody when you tried to make your way across the floor. The offense wasn't all that h'important, don't you see. The trial's the thing. Somebody acts as judge, you see, with a knotted towel on 'is 'ead to be a wig. And twelve men get picked to act as jurors. It's all very entertaining, don't you see, with the barrister addressing the cove in the towel as m'lord and the jurors taking it all in. Entertaining, that is, for everybody but the poor sod—begging your pardon, miss—who's standing trial. But the main point of the exercise, you see, is that the defendant is found guilty and then fined. Only this time they didn't know their man, for Mr. Slaughter refused to pay up."

"Well, I should think not!" Miss Osborne observed indignantly.

"Well, you've 'ad no h'experience of the consequences if that's your way of thinking." Mr. Crake paused to shudder. "Anyhow, Mr. Slaughter was found guilty as charged, and when 'e refused to pay, 'e was sentenced to the stocks, which in h'actuality means they put the poor devil's 'ead through the legs of a chair and stretch out 'is arms and tie 'em. Only Mr. Slaughter remarked, while looking at those clean fingernails of 'is, cool as anything, that 'e wasn't inclined to accept the punishment either. And that's when they set out to make 'im do it.

"I'm 'ere to tell you that they cleared a space in 'alf a tick, with all the rest of us bug-eyed bastards—beg pardon, miss—pressing up against the walls to miss the mayhem. And Charley Crews— the biggest, the meanest, of that scurvy lot, wot 'ad choked the life out of 'is own brother who'd annoyed 'im—was appointed the enforcer. Well, 'e 'eaded toward Mr. Slaughter in a kind of crouch, meaning to squeeze compliance out of 'im with those brute arms of 'is. But before you could say 'Jack Robinson,' Crews was stretched out on the floor from the prettiest left hook to the jaw that you could imagine.

"Pity was, it didn't do for the big brute. And as for the rest, it wasn't pretty. Crews got to 'is feet, none the worse for wear, not 'aving really enough sense to 'ave it knocked out of 'im but just enough to figure 'e'd h'underestimated the enemy and to arm 'imself this time with a broken gin bottle. Well, like I just said, the rest wasn't pretty, miss, and I'll spare you the gory details. Suffice it to say that though Mr. Slaughter got carved up pretty bad in the process and was bleedin' like a curst stuck pig, at the end of it all Charley Crews was laid out cold on the floor like the felled ox he most resembled."

"Oh, dear God." Jervis was as white as the shirt points that framed his face. "That new scar on his face!"

"Which is nothing compared to the one on his chest," Eliza chimed in. "It's truly horrible—all long and jagged."

Both men looked at her in some astonishment and she reddened. "But surely he was able to move out of there the next day," she said to cover her embarrassment.

"That's just wot 'e didn't do." Mr. Crake smiled in remembrance. "You see, at that point, 'e 'ad a reputation. Why, big Charley Crews, when they finally brought 'im to, was the first to admit 'e'd been beaten fair and square and became 'is staunchest friend. And though Mr. Slaughter never said so aloud, it was plain as a pikestaff 'e'd decided to put 'is blunt to better use. Wot 'e h'actually did say was 'ow he liked the society we offered.

" 'E knew, don't you see, that 'e could survive the place. But there was many as 'ad no hope of making

116

it. Did you know as 'ow they put mere boys in there alongside the rest of us? Well, Mr. Slaughter began to run a regular stage line, you might say, bribing those youngsters' way out of the place. 'E took care of a few grown men as well who obviously 'adn't much stomach for the accommodations. Oh, 'e 'ad to fight a few more battles afore 'e was done, all of which I'm 'appy to report 'e won. But none of 'em was 'alf so glorious as putting out the lights of Charley Crews. Why, your Savage Stenhouse can't 'old a candle to big Charley. So that's why I was telling you to put your blunt on Mr. Slaughter." He nodded judiciously, having gone full circle.

"I don't believe in wagering," Eliza said virtuously. "And I don't believe in two men pounding themselves to death for the amusement of a bloodthirsty crowd." She looked a trifle ill. "I'd give anything to be able to stop it."

"Oh, I don't think you could do that, miss. No matter 'ow close you and Mr. Slaughter may be." Mr. Crake was obviously recalling her familiarity with a certain torso. " 'E's got to get little Edwin Potts a place at Mr. Newman's."

"Who the deuce is Edwin Potts? And what exactly is Mr. Newman's place?" Jervis asked while Eliza was simultaneously inquiring, "And why does Edwin—whoever he is—need to be sent to wherever?"

"Edwin Potts is a nine-year-old pickpocket that joined the Newgate fraternity 'bout a week afore Mr. Slaughter and meself left it. Did I mention that 'im and me shook the dust of the place orf our boots on the same day? Anyhow, little Edwin was caught separating some gentry cove from 'is pocket watch. The little runt took up the trade, don't you see, as a step up from chimney sweeping, which wasn't to say 'e 'ad a real aptitude for that particular calling. The thing was, 'e'd got a little tired of 'aving the bottoms of 'is feet singed, seein' as 'ow 'e was afraid to climb. But 'is former occupation left 'im decidedly weak in the lungs, and Mr. Slaughter was afeared that long confinement in that place would kill the lad, always supposing the inmates didn't do it first because of 'is coughing keeping 'em awake o' nights.

"So before Mr. Slaughter bid good-bye to Newgate, 'e 'ad the boy transferred to the state side. Wot you might call the admission fee there is three guineas, with ten and sixpence a week more for a single bed. But Mr. Slaughter went even further and got four beds for the lad, which is the same as saying he gets a private room. And now 'e's after the prize money from the mill to provide the tyke with a room at Mr. Newman's. Which would be the same as putting up at an inn, I'd say, except for the fact you ain't allowed to leave it."

"Who is Mr. Newman?" Eliza repeated.

"Lor', miss, 'e's the gaoler." Mr. Crake seemed amazed that everyone didn't know that. "And 'e's accommodated some of 'is Majesty's most distinguished prisoners in 'is time. The Marquess of Sligo, to name but one. But Mr. Newman's accommodations don't come cheap by any means. And today's prize money could provide a trust fund, in a manner of speaking, to keep the lad in comfort till 'e's a grown man and then some, which is wot 'is Majesty's justice 'as in mind for 'im. And I'm in charge of the fund," he added proudly. "Mr. Slaughter 'as asked me down to carry the winnings back up to London and make all the arrangements. Not that I wouldn't've come anyhow. For I've been raising a bit of blunt on me own account, you see, to place on Mr. Slaughter. Didn't want to waste a penny of it on coach fare. For at the odds they'll be giving, I should do well, very well, indeed."

Eliza's eyes grew moist. "Little Edwin is fortunate to have a friend like you, sir."

Mr. Crake looked a bit embarrassed. "Oh, Lor'

luv you, miss, me own investment ain't for Edwin Potts. The tyke will be well enough provided for. Mr. Slaughter's seeing to that, right and tight. It's me own depleted reserves I mean to remedy."

"Oh." There didn't seem to be much else to say.

"And like I was suggesting, you folk should 'ave a bit of a flutter. For take it from me, Mr. Slaughter's a regular lion-heart. If 'e don't do for the Savage, well, I'm a Dutchman."

They were now approaching the field set aside for the mill and their pace had once more slowed down to a crawl. Mr. Crake thanked them profusely for the respite given to his boot soles but concluded he'd be quicker now on foot. Again urging them to put their blunt on Mr. Slaughter, he jumped down from the tiger's perch and, with a wave of farewell, disappeared into the crowd pressing toward the ring.

"We should have given him some money to wager for us." Eliza appeared to have changed her mind on the evils of gambling. "For little Edwin, I mean."

"And do you think we'd ever have seen him again if we had?"

"Certainly." She bristled. "If Garrick Slaughter can trust him to take his winnings back to Newgate, we surely can."

"You swallowed his story, then, did you?"

"Of course I believed him. Didn't you? I'd seen those scars, remember? Oh, don't look so Friday-faced. Can I help it if Mr. Slaughter removed his shirt to wash in the inn yard? The whole world saw him. Anyhow, I believe that everything Mr. Crake said was true."

"Oh, I believe him about the fights." Jervis was looking a bit ill at the memory. "And about little Edwin. All that's just like Garrick. What I ain't so inclined to swallow, though, is Mr. Crake's role in

119

the whole business. He may or may not be in charge of little Edwin's fund.''

"Why on earth should he make up such a story?''

"How the deuce would I know? To look important. Or to get us to hand over our money for him to punt—like you almost did.''

His tone reminded her of another lecture she'd been given on being too trusting, on being a flat. "Well, he didn't insist, did he?'' she said defensively.

"No, but all the same I'll take charge of our betting if you don't mind.''

Eliza held her tongue at that point, not wishing to distract him. He was weaving in and out among the other vehicles with a speed and skill that she found as admirable as it was unnerving. "I think this is the best we can hope to do'' was his comment after he'd squeezed between a high-perch phaeton and a chaise into a space that she would have sworn was too narrow by half to accommodate them.

They were at the top of an incline that formed a natural amphitheater. The grass of the slope was still wet from an early-morning shower, and the greater part of the level field at its base was plowed up by the trampling of a multitude of fight fanatics. Exempted from this muddied state was one small area enclosed by stakes and ropes. The battleground remained a virgin green.

"Wish we had that,'' Jervis whispered as he stared enviously at the high-perch phaeton. "I don't know how much we'll be able to see from here. Maybe when the mill starts we can squeeze through the crowd and get right up next to the ring.''

"I don't think that's a very good idea.'' A dry voice spoke behind them. The startled twosome turned around to stare down into the disapproving, tight-lipped face of the Viscount Wenham.

Chapter Fifteen

"*I hope you will not blame Jervis—Mr. Wenham,* I meant to say—for bringing me here."

Eliza, feeling most uncomfortable in the presence of this elegantly dressed, silver-haired gentleman, was seated inside his lordship's carriage where he had insisted on taking her.

"This really is no place for a young lady," he'd chided. "And if you are seen by any of our acquaintances, I think it's far better that you seem to be with me and not my rackety son." Jervis had gone off rather sulkily to place their bets and Eliza felt it incumbent upon herself to make some sort of explanation.

"I'm afraid I rather insisted upon coming."

"You are a boxing enthusiast, Miss Osborne? I must say it's an unusual interest for a female."

"No, of course not. I think the sport, if you can call it that, is odious. I just happen to have a particular interest in this mill. But it has nothing to do with Jervis, except that he was coming and I couldn't come alone. But he has not the slightest interest in me, let me assure you."

"No?" Lord Wenham's eyebrows rose. "Then may I say that this is one of the very few times I've been disappointed in him."

Eliza gave his lordship a suspicious look, but his eyes were twinkling. "And let me also assure you," she continued, "that I'm not setting my cap for him, if that's what you're thinking."

"Well, I find that a pity, too. But, unlike my wife, I never thought you were. And by the by, I wish to apologize on her behalf for the accusations she made."

"Her ladyship told you about that, did she? And did she also send you here to keep an eye on Jervis?"

"No, to both your questions. First, I don't think Charlotte would be eager to speak of an incident that hardly reflected to her credit. And neither she nor I knew that Jervis was coming here. Actually, I learned of your interview with my wife from one of the servants. We keep little of our lives hidden from those who look after us, you know."

Eliza nodded sagaciously, thinking of Betty.

"Through the same source I came to realize it's not Jervis but my other son you're interested in."

Eliza did hope she had not just been put to the blush, but she feared the worst. "Oh, I'm interested in Mr. Slaughter right enough, but not in the way I think you mean. I'm interested enough to pray he doesn't get killed today. And, frankly, sir, I don't quite see how you have the gall to come watch this. For if he does come to harm, well, it's all your fault."

"My fault?" The chilly look Lord Wenham now gave Eliza served as a reminder of their respective stations. "I hardly see how I can be held responsible for Garrick's attraction to this admittedly brutal sport."

"The attraction, as you call it, is money. And he wouldn't need it so desperately if you hadn't disinherited him."

"And what makes you suppose I've done so?" His lordship's tone lowered the coach temperature by several degrees.

"Why, it's common knowledge. And, yes, come to think on it, Lady Cheselden did mention it, I believe."

"Lady Cheselden, Miss Osborne, is an elderly lady who entertains some very odd fancies. She's hardly a reliable source where my personal business is concerned. Now perhaps you'd best tell me just why Garrick is in such desperate need of money."

Eliza did so, repeating almost word for word what Mr. Crake had told them, sparing him no detail of the Newgate horrors, and winding up with the plight of little Edwin Potts. She had begun the story gladly, feeling it was time his lordship learned a few home truths about all the hardships his natural son had had to endure, but as the proud man crumbled before her eyes she soon lost all relish for the narration.

"Oh, my God," he whispered when she'd concluded, more to himself than to her. "I'd thought to spare him all of that. I had no idea. Oh, I knew a little of what prison was like, though not the full horror of it. But I knew enough to realize you could buy your way into tolerable quarters, so I sent funds expressly for that. I had no idea he'd not used them." His voice broke. "The damned, quixotic fool.

"Oh, I do blame myself for this whole business, Miss Osborne," he continued bitterly. "You can rest assured on that score. I see now that I was always too hard on the lad. But my position wasn't easy. I would like to have acknowledged him, but it couldn't be. And so I thought it best that he make his own way as far as possible, learn to be self-reliant. Now I can see that I was wrong. I should have sent him to school like a gentleman's son. Instead, he was a king's scholar. Garrick is very clever, you know." A note of pride had crept into his voice. "But those scholarship lads led a wretched life. Good preparation for Newgate, no doubt," he ended bitterly.

Eliza could think of nothing appropriate to say and for once did not go on and say something, anyway. Lord Wenham hardly seemed aware of her as he continued his self-flagellation.

"What I blame myself for most is that when he came to our London house asking for a loan to help his friend, I turned him down. But he was quite drunk, you see. And I certainly was not prepared to deal with him in that condition. And he should have come to me privately. The entire household was overhearing the business."

"What you mean, sir, is that Lady Wenham was within earshot and you knew she would not approve."

Eliza expected to be struck dead for such audacity. Instead, he looked more ill than he had before, if that were possible.

"You can hardly blame a wife for disliking a man's love child. And Charlotte has always had a completely irrational jealousy of Garrick. She views him as some sort of threat to her own son. Which is absurd. Even if she mistrusts me, the law would see to Jervis's interests. But you're right, of course. The fact that Charlotte was overhearing our interview undoubtedly made me act differently than I would have done otherwise. That and the fact that Garrick had shot the cat to a degree I could not approve of. Garrick ran with a rackety crowd in London. But I'd not heard of his being castaway before. It seemed totally out of character. Though hardly as far out of character as theft." His face contorted. "I understand that he'd been crossed in love somehow, which could, I suppose, explain his condition if not excuse it. And as for taking the earrings, well, I collect that in his drunken fog he believed himself entitled to more from me. Which, too, is an explanation, but never an excuse. There can be no excuse for such . . . ungentlemanly behavior."

"And you are convinced that he took them?"

"Of course. There was never any doubt of that."

"There is in his mind."

"Can you blame him?" Lord Wenham looked past her through the carriage window, seeing nothing. "It can't be easy for a proud man to accept that he's done something so reprehensible. Besides, his mind was fogged, remember."

"It can't be easy," she retorted, "for an equally proud man to entertain the possibility that someone in his household could have wished to disgrace his natural son and therefore put the gems in Mr. Slaughter's pocket."

Lord Wenham's eyes impaled her. "You go too far, Miss Osborne. What you are saying is impossible. More than that—unthinkable. I realize that you're in love with Garrick, but for your own sake, as well as for the reputation of my family, you should not weave fantasies."

It was just as well that Jervis appeared then at the window to say that their bets were placed. "Now see here, sir"—he reacted to the tense atmosphere— "I do hope that you, too, haven't been reading the 'riot act' to Miss Osborne. Her being here with me isn't at all what you think."

"On the contrary, my boy, it's the other way around. Miss Osborne has been reading the 'riot act' to me."

Lord Wenham turned to Eliza. "But I am sorry, Miss Osborne, if I've said anything to offend you. I think both my sons are fortunate to have you for a friend." He opened the coach door for her. "The bout will begin at any moment and you'll wish to get back to your vantage post."

"I've been wondering, sir," Jervis blurted out as he took Eliza's hand to help her down, "just why you happened to be here. I mean to say"—he reddened—"I didn't think you went in for this sort of thing."

"Didn't you? And here I'd thought of myself as a regular sporting cove." He smiled, but Jervis only looked more puzzled. "Oh, well, then, let's just say that Miss Osborne and I share a similar interest in this particular mill. But pray keep in mind, Jervis, you've done an imprudent thing in bringing her here. If she should be made to feel uncomfortable, escort her back here immediately."

"My God, Eliza, did you hear what he actually said?" Jervis breathed as they hurried toward his curricle as fast as the crowd and his affliction would allow.

"To bring me back if I feel uncomfortable. But I assure you—"

"Not that, pea-goose. He actually said to 'both my sons.' He never did a thing like that even before Garrick disgraced himself. And since then . . . Well, it's been as if Garrick's dead."

"And does that put your nose out of joint?" Eliza had reverted to suspecting everyone.

"Do you know, I really should *make* you go back to the coach for a remark like that." Jervis spoke pleasantly enough, but the hoist he gave her into his rig almost sent her sprawling.

"Oh, do hurry!" she exclaimed as she regained her balance. "They're coming. The mill's about to start."

Indeed, the sea of spectators crowded around the ring parted to provide a path. And down it strode—no, rolled along—an enormous, knock-kneed man wearing, despite the heat, an open greatcoat, through which it was possible to see his bare, barreled chest matted with coarsely curling hair.

"Oh, my goodness, look at the size of him!" Eliza clutched Jervis's arm and tried to think of David and Goliath as the crowd broke into a thunderous roar in honor of the champion. He raised a hamlike fist in salute, then paused and turned expectantly.

"Maybe he's changed his mind." Eliza spoke hopefully when the challenger was slow to appear. A few impatient spectators resorted to catcalls.

"Not him," Jervis replied. "You have to remember that on his mother's side he comes from an acting family. He plans to make an entrance."

And sure enough, just as the mounting tension grew too much to bear, Garrick Slaughter came sauntering nonchalantly down the human walkway. "Would you look at that?" Jervis breathed while the crowd hip-hip-hip-hoo-rahed.

The challenger might have been out for a stroll down Bond Street. He was wearing a long-tailed coat of dark blue superfine that was trimmed with a double row of silver buttons. His white waistcoat was piped in red. An impeccable white starcher wound intricately just below his stiff shirt points. He was wearing soft leather gloves and carried an ebony cane topped with a knob of gleaming silver. Indeed, his only concession to the day's activity was that he wore a pair of white knee-smalls rather than the more fashionable pantaloons.

Mr. Slaughter ambled up to the mammoth champion, doffed his hat with a grin and a bow, then sent the modish tall-crowned beaver sailing into the ring. It was followed by more delighted whoops from the packed watchers.

There was something almost sinuous, at least to Eliza's way of thinking, in the slow, deliberate way that Garrick Slaughter began to strip, while the burly champion, who only had to shed a greatcoat, stood disdainfully by.

He first peeled off his gloves, finger by finger, then flicked a speck of dust off one sleeve with the white leather. Next, he shrugged out of his form-fitted coat and folded it carefully while the crowd chuckled with delight. He tossed the bundle to a spectator whom Eliza and Jervis simultaneously recognized as Mr. Crake. After that he removed his waistcoat, taking each button with the same studied deliberation.

"Told you he was a showman," Jervis said.

"Are you sure he's not just stalling for time?" Eliza's nerves were stretched to the snapping point.

"Don't think so, but, by God, I would be. Do you reckon that cove he milled down in prison was actually that huge?" Jervis had now voiced the unthinkable, and Eliza shuddered.

Garrick was shedding his white linen shirt now and the crowd was heard to gasp. The long, jagged, vicious scar was clearly visible.

"That's . . . terrible!" exclaimed Jervis.

"Didn't I say so?"

"Well, at least they can't use bottles here."

The combatants were climbing into the ring now, where they shook hands ceremoniously. There were shouts of "Down in front there!" and the spectators around the ring obligingly sat on the trampled grass, and the mill began.

At first the two boxers circled one another warily, their arms upraised in the classic defensive pose, their bare knuckles gleaming. Then Savage Stenhouse lunged at the smaller man, his fists flying.

"Look out!" Eliza's scream was drowned out by the crowd's roar as Garrick deftly sidestepped the onslaught and landed a punishing facer to the champion's jaw.

"My God!" Jervis croaked. "Did you see that?

Might as well have been a flea bite. That blow would have felled any normal man."

The champion had merely backed away and looked insulted. He was now viewing his assailant with a malevolent eye.

"He doesn't have enough brain to rattle, I'm sure of it." Eliza screamed once more as the Savage mounted another offensive.

"Stop that, will you!" Jervis snapped. "This is bad enough without you screeching in my ear. I should have known better than to bring a curst female to a boxing mill."

"I'm sorry." Eliza looked contrite. "I'll do better. I promise it." And, true, she was soon bereft of speech as the battle in the ring began in earnest.

When the two at last backed off, blood streamed down Garrick Slaughter's face from the opened scar above his eye. One of the four men inside the ring (two officials and an assistant for each boxer, Eliza had surmised when she'd recognized Garrick's groom and sparring partner) sponged it off, and the fight continued. As far as appearances went, the champion was still unscathed. "Oh, Lord, this is awful," Jervis muttered.

From that moment on things began to blur as first one man and then the other went crashing to the ground, and Eliza concentrated on not becoming sick. And at the point when Garrick's nose as well as his forehead streamed blood, she was glad to follow Jervis's barked command, "Don't look!"

After that she judged the progress of the fight by Jervis's outcries while she studiously studied the toes of her soft leather shoes.

"One of his lamps is out!" he whooped, and she croaked back, "What *are* you talking about?"

"Garrick's closed one of the Savage's eyes," he answered impatiently. "That should help a bit." Eliza counted backwards as she grew more queasy.

When at those moments during the interminable

fight she screwed up enough courage to take a look, she knew with a mounting despair that Garrick could never take such punishment and live. It was nothing short of a miracle that he was still on his feet, bobbing and weaving, trying to dodge the worst of the furious onslaught and to land some punches of his own.

It was a gallant effort, as the roars of the appreciative audience made clear. But the outcome was all too predictable. There was simply too much brute strength to be overcome. And the champion was well named. She averted her head once more as the Savage's powerful fist drew back, then cannonballed toward its target.

She heard the sickening crack as bone and flesh encountered bone and flesh, then the collective gasp that was quickly transposed into a roar that bounced off the carriages and sent the horses rearing in their harnesses.

"He's done it! He's done it! He's done it!" Jervis was whooping and jumping up and down like a demented India-rubber ball, his afflicted foot forgotten in his frenzy. "He's done it, you widgeon! Don't you understand, he's done it!" He pulled the bewildered Eliza up from the carriage seat and hugged her ecstatically. "He's knocked the Savage out! He's won! Garrick's beaten the champion! For God's sake, look happy, you little pea-goose!"

"Are you sure?" Eliza was staring toward the ring around which the spectators were leaping and whooping like wild American Indians. And true, Savage Stenhouse was stretched out on the grass and his attendant was dousing him with water. But there was no look of victory about the figure who was clinging to the ropes like a drowning man clutching a lifeline. It was the only thing keeping him from the champion's prone fate.

"Where the devil do you think you're going?" Jervis yelled as Eliza scrambled down from the curricle. "Have you gone daft?" he yelped. "Papa will kill me. Come back here!" He chased down the incline after her as fast as his clubfoot and the frenzied, jostling crowd would allow.

A phalanx of bruisers were pushing the throng back from ringside. "Now lookee 'ere, miss," one bellowed as Eliza ducked underneath his arm and through the ropes. He did manage to collar Jervis, however, who croaked, "Let me go, you brute! I'm Slaughter's brother. And," he added in a desperate rush of inspiration, "that's our sister looking after him."

"Good Lord, is it really you, or am I seeing things?" Garrick shook his head to try to clear it as Eliza took the wet towel from the astonished groom and began to dab tenderly at his face.

"Yes, it's me all right," she answered grimly, "and you're not seeing things. You couldn't possibly. Both your eyes are swelling shut. Oh, Garrick, how could you do this?"

"How could I do this?" he answered thickly. "The question is, how could you do such a hare-brained thing as to come to a place like this? Traveling alone on the Brighton stage doesn't even touch it for impropriety."

"I'm sorry, Garrick." Jervis, too, had obtained a towel and was rendering aid. "I know I shouldn't have brought her, but I never dreamed the silly goose would go and climb into the ring."

"Well, get her out of here. Never mind about me, lad. Eliza, if I had the strength left," he added weakly as he let go of the ropes and eased down upon the grass, "I'd ring a peal over you."

"Here, let me through," an imperious voice demanded. His aristocratic mien won Lord Wenham easy access to the ring. "Oh, my dear boy." He knelt down beside the prone Garrick. "What has he done to you?"

"Put my daylights out for one thing. Is that you,

sir? If I'm not knocked silly, this must be a regular convention. Sorry I can't see it."

"Don't try to talk. Let's get you home. Robert!" he called to the burly coachman who'd elbowed his way to ringside. "Here, give us a hand."

"I've got a horse here somewhere."

"I admire your rosy outlook, Garrick, if you expected to ride home."

"I take it, then, that you didn't put your blunt on me, sir." The attempt at a smile made all his watchers wince.

"As a matter of fact, I did."

"Well, I'm damned. Oh, is Eliza still here? Somebody see to her."

Then, after some mumbled instructions to the groom about passing his winnings along to Barnaby Crake, Garrick submitted to being led away, though he resisted being carried. "Hate to look in worse shape than the Savage, don't you know," he said as he pulled himself up painfully by the rope.

The crowd still thronged, cheering lustily, as he walked through it unassisted except for his father's hand upon his arm to guide him.

Eliza and Jervis collected their own bets and with no discussion of the matter went to find Mr. Crake at ringside and hand their winnings over. Shortly thereafter, they were once again in a press of carriages, this time heading away from Brighton.

Both were subdued. Conversation was desultory. Once Eliza broke a lengthy silence to inquire, "Do you think he'll be all right?"

"Bound to be." Jervis's voice almost carried conviction. "Don't think anything's broken. Just battered, that's all."

"He looked . . . ghastly."

"Well, it's nothing compared to the way he's going to look."

"Thank you very much."

"No need getting testy. Truth's truth."

They logged in several more miles then without speaking until they were almost home. The road was now deserted. This time it was Jervis who broke the silence. "Eliza, let's get married."

"What did you say?" With an effort she came out of her reverie, then turned to gape at him. "What *did* you say?"

"You heard me. I said, let's get married."

"What's the matter with you? Have you taken leave of your wits? You aren't the one who was battered senseless in the ring, you know."

"Now don't go flying off into the boughs till you've heard me out, for God's sake. I'm perfectly serious. I've been thinking of nothing else since we left the fight, and it's a famous notion actually."

"It's a bird-witted notion."

"It is not. Now listen, dammit. Unless I do something drastic—and quick—I'm going to find myself married to Juliet."

"Well, isn't that what you want?"

"Never mind about that just now. The only point is, it's not what she wants. It's Garrick she's in love with."

Suddenly, Eliza felt very tired. The day's drama had left her drained. "Did she say so?" she managed to ask.

"She doesn't have to," he answered impatiently. "Who wouldn't be in love with Garrick?"

The question really was a poser. She didn't try to answer it.

"The man's a nonesuch," he added.

Well, he'd get no argument from her on that point, either. "Still," she did manage to say, "in the world's eyes he's also a thief. So Juliet won't be allowed to marry him. No use being a martyr for nothing."

Jervis's face was filled with misery as he turned to face her for the first time. His voice shook. "Do you think I could possibly marry the woman Garrick's in love with after all that he's been through? I just couldn't do it, that's all. I thought you'd understand."

"Yes, I collect I do. Though I'm not sure your sacrifice will do him any good."

"That's not the point. I just simply couldn't live with myself."

"I do see that. But there's no use making a bad matter worse, you know. You don't have to immolate yourself to the extent of marrying me." She managed a halfhearted smile.

They had been tooling along at a rapid pace. He now slowed his team to rest it. "This is no time for funning. I'm dead serious. The God's truth is, if I don't head this thing off by already being married, Mama will wear me down till I offer for Juliet. She's longing to announce our betrothal at my coming-of-age. And as for immolation, that's fustian. The fact of the matter is, we'd deal well together. Why, if I'd never met Juliet, I'd be offering for you anyhow, I'll bet a monkey."

"Th-thank you very much." Eliza laughed.

"Oh, the devil." He grinned. "I really botched that, didn't I? But you do know what I mean. I like you enormously."

"You do not. You can barely abide me. We've been at daggers drawn ever since we met."

"But that's just it. I'm comfortable with you, don't you understand? I've never met anyone I'm so at ease with. Why, I don't even mind my clumsy foot when I'm around you."

"Thank you, Jervis." She was truly touched. "And I like you prodigiously, too." She was rather amazed to find that she spoke the truth. "But that's not enough for us to marry on."

"You think not? It's a devil of a lot more than most leg-shackled couples manage, I'll tell you. But I do see what you mean, of course. But who's to say that the other part wouldn't come later? We haven't tried, you know."

And before Eliza could even dream of his intent, let alone voice a protest, he had taken her rather awkwardly in his arms and they were bumping noses.

"Oh, the devil with this thing!" He untied the ribbons of her straw bonnet, the brim of which closely framed her face, and tossed it on the floor. This time the kiss was right on target.

He was a quick learner. She'd give him that much. What had started out as a pretty tame affair soon gained enough momentum that she felt it incumbent upon herself to give him a stiff shove that nearly shot him off the carriage seat.

"See what I mean?" He grinned.

"I certainly do," she gasped. "But it changes nothing. I'll not marry you. The idea's preposterous."

"No it ain't." He clucked at his bays, which were still plodding along with slackened reins. "And when you think on it a bit, you're bound to have a change of heart."

"I'll do no such thing," she retorted stoutly while resolutely pushing a sudden vision of Warleigh Hall and of herself, a viscountess, firmly from her mind.

Chapter Sixteen

An invitation card to a ball celebrating the Honorable Jervis Wenham's coming-of-age arrived at the vicarage the next morning. When Betty brought it in, the household was at the breakfast table. Mr. Tomkins handed it to Mrs. Tomkins with a smile.

"But how wonderful!" she exclaimed, her eyes wide with surprise. "I had not thought to be asked to the dinner before the ball as well."

"Whyever not?" Mr. Tomkins buttered a light wig complacently. "We are, after all, part of the family."

"Yes, but the relationship is not a close one. Do you know, I'll bet a monkey it's because of Eliza."

"Tsk, tsk. You, of all people, should not use cant phrases, m'dear." The vicar looked pained, whether at his wife's lapse in language or at the slight to his own consequence, it was impossible to say.

"Oh, I do beg your pardon. It's difficult *always* to be a parson's wife—even in private."

"I know, m'dear." The vicar smiled and kissed her on the forehead as he left the table. "But at any rate, I'm pleased if you're pleased about the ball—*and* the dinner. Now I'm off for my conference with the sexton."

The door had barely closed behind him when Mrs. Tomkins gave her niece an impish look. "I still bet a monkey we owe the invitation to you, m'dear. You've become such a favorite of . . . Lady Cheselden." For some unknown reason she seemed to think she'd said something witty and giggled like a schoolgirl over her tea.

But then she grew quite serious. "I expect you think I've been very remiss in my duties, Eliza dear."

"But how ridiculous. Just because you used a cant expression? Why, I cannot imagine a better wife for a vicar than you are."

"Oh, I don't mean that." Mrs. Tomkins waved away the parish. "I was referring to my duties toward you. You may recall that I had meant to find some suitable young man for you. Well, I've quite failed to do so."

"You mustn't worry about that. In fact, I'm actually relieved. There's nothing worse than being obliged to charm some poor gentleman who's been cajoled into presenting himself for inspection. But if you're determined to feel a failure unless you expose me to the other sex, cheer up. I'm sure the cream of Sussex will be at the ball."

"That's certainly true." Mrs. Tomkins brightened. "But to be perfectly candid, the reason I haven't done more to 'cajole' gentlemen into presenting themselves for inspection, as you put it, is that you seemed to have your hands full with Lord Wenham's sons."

Eliza choked on her bread and butter.

"Oh, you mustn't think I'm being a busybody, m'dear. You see, a vicar's wife is in everyone's confidence. And not much is missed in a small community.

"I can't say I approve of the rather clandestine manner of your meetings, nor would your papa, not to mention the dear vicar," she said with a shudder, "but they are both remarkable young gentlemen. Of course, Mr. Garrick Slaughter is rather under a cloud these days. I know my brother will think little of me for not nipping such an unsuitable friendship in the bud. But I must own I've always had a soft spot in my heart for him. Why, when—"

Eliza interrupted the flow to say firmly, "Pray excuse me, Aunt, but I must tell you that you quite mistake the nature of my relationship to Mr. Wenham and Mr. Slaughter. We are friends, no more." She repressed an urge to tell her relative about Jervis's proposal. "In point of fact, they are both in love with Lady Juliet."

"Well, now, there's only one of her, is there not?"

"Aunt Hester! If you think that I am prepared to snap up her ladyship's leavings, I'll have you know—"

Her tirade was cut short by the entrance of the maid, who informed them that Lady Juliet Greenwood had walked down from the Hall to see Miss Eliza and was waiting in the drawing room.

"Oh, my goodness," Mrs. Tomkins whispered to Eliza, her eyes wide, "do you think she heard?"

"Couldn't've," Betty interposed. "Have to stand right up next to this door if you hope to hear anything. It's ever so thick, you see."

"Be thankful for small mercies," Mrs. Tomkins breathed piously. "Now run along, child. Don't keep your guest waiting. And, Betty, see if her ladyship would like some tea."

"Prefers lemonade. I just asked her." On that Parthian shot the maid bustled from the room.

As she hurried into the drawing room and greeted her guest, it struck Eliza anew, with a rather dampening effect upon her spirits, just how lovely Lady Juliet was. Even though her face was rather flushed from the exertion of her walk and the heat of the morning—or perhaps because of it—she was a vision to make every other female long to take a mallet to her own looking glass.

The servant must have been of the same opinion. She came into the room on Eliza's heels intent on memorizing every feature of Lady Juliet's face to the peril of the lemonade and pound cake she carried.

"Thank you," Eliza said pointedly to cut off the stare. Betty then plopped the silver tray on a small rosewood table next to the guest's chair and reluctantly withdrew, leaving the door ajar behind her. Eliza walked over to close it.

"I hope I haven't disturbed you, Miss Osborne," her ladyship apologized. "I realize it's early, but I was out for exercise and the temptation to stop by the vicarage for a visit with you quite overcame me."

If, as Eliza suspected, Lady Juliet had some ulterior motive for her visit, it was slow in manifesting itself. Eliza poured the lemonade and served the cake, trying to think of a conversation topic they might have in common aside from the obvious ones. "My aunt and uncle and I are eagerly looking forward to Lord and Lady Wenham's ball" was what she finally came up with as she took a seat opposite her guest.

"Are you, indeed? I wish that I were."

"You mean you aren't?" Eliza stared across her glass in amazement. "I would think you'd be delighted. You're bound to be the belle of all such occasions."

Lady Juliet shrugged off the compliment. "It's Jervis—Mr. Wenham, that is—I'm thinking of. He does not dance. Because of his foot, you know."

"Oh, but I'm sure he'll not object if you do."

"But that's hardly the point, is it?" Lady Juliet's expression came as close to looking severe as those lovely features would allow it. "My concern is that he not be made to feel uncomfortable. He's very sensitive, you know."

"Well, yes, I suppose so. About his limp at any rate."

"You do seem to know Mr. Wenham quite well, don't you, Miss Osborne."

Though her ladyship's tone was offhand, Eliza had the distinct impression that she was fishing. "Oh, no, I would not say so," she equivocated. "My acquaintance with Mr. Wenham is slight. I'm by no means a judge of his sensitivity. I agree, though, that if he dislikes it above all things, a ball seems a peculiar way to celebrate his coming-of-age."

"That's exactly what he said to Lady Wenham. But her answer was that a ball is traditional and to do otherwise would only call attention to his infirmity."

"Fiddlesticks!"

"Oh, I could not agree more. For if you ask me, Miss Osborne, I believe his mother to be at fault where Jervis's infirmity is concerned. If she did not view it as such a tragedy, he would be much the better for it." There was something in the set of her face at that moment that reminded Eliza of the donkeys on the bridge. She wondered if Lady Wenham was aware of the streak of stubbornness in Lady Juliet. She might not prove to be as malleable a daughter as her ladyship imagined. Eliza found this amazing bit of insight oddly cheering. She started woolgathering for a moment, thinking of its implications, until her guest brought her back to the present by clearing her throat delicately. "Had you heard, Miss Osborne," she lowered her voice and leaned closer to speak confidentially, "that Mr. Slaughter has been hurt?"

"Why, er, yes. That is, I understand that he took part in a mill—a boxing match, I mean." She looked at Lady Juliet warily, wondering just how much of the previous day's history she was aware of. "How did you come to know of it?"

"Jervis told me. Oh, Miss Osborne, it is the saddest, most touching story. Mr. Slaughter was almost killed doing battle for a poor, unfortunate child in prison. Really, the way Jervis told the story, it was the most noble thing imaginable." Her eyes glowed.

"I'm sure it must have been." Eliza felt her way cautiously, still having no notion of how inclusive Jervis's account had been.

"But then I expect that Jervis had already told you about the Newgate child."

"About Master Potts? No, I did not hear about him through Mr. Wenham." She fell back upon the literal truth while sidestepping the issue. For she had come to the conclusion that the purpose of Lady Juliet's visit was to probe the nature of her relationship with Jervis. And if so, that implied at least a mild kind of jealousy that spoke well of Jervis's chances with the beauty. Perhaps he was the one she'd choose anyhow, even if Garrick Slaughter became eligible. Lady Juliet's next remark, however, brought this sanguine bit of speculation to an end. "Really, Miss Osborne, I was not able to sleep a wink last night for thinking of poor Mr. Slaughter's sufferings."

"You weren't?" Eliza offered her ladyship more cake.

"No, indeed." Lady Juliet accepted a slice and took a dainty bite. "For as Jervis described him, he must be in the most agonizing pain." Her lovely green eyes grew moist with tears.

"I should have thought Mr. Wenham would have wished to spare you the gory details." Eliza sounded rather waspish to her own ears.

"Oh, pray don't be too hard on him. For he is most desirous that I shouldn't think too harshly of Mr. Slaughter for that one, terrible lapse, don't you see." She paused delicately. "You were, perhaps, aware that they are half brothers?"

"Yes."

Lady Juliet's face, which had recovered from her exercise sometime before, had grown rosy once again. "I thought as much. Mama can't get over the fact, nor can I, that such a delicate matter seems so generally known in this neighborhood. It does not seem at all the thing."

"No, I collect not. But there are few secrets in the country."

"Well, it's most uncomfortable. I much preferred it when Mr. Slaughter was merely a doctor's son, which, while hardly of the first stare, was certainly respectable. But, still, I must confess that I find Jervis's loyalty to his disgraced half brother touching. No, I'll go even further. There's something altogether noble in such an attitude."

Eliza was having difficulty seeing Jervis in this noble light, but for once she thought it more politic to smile noncommittally than to say so.

"But as I was saying, I am deeply distressed for Mr. Slaughter's sufferings. Which is, in part, why I've come to see you, Miss Osborne."

And while Eliza watched with fascination, Lady Juliet reached into the bosom of her walking dress and pulled out a folded piece of paper. "I have here a remedy my family swears by. A salve especially beneficial for sore eyes. I understand that both of his have been closed by that monster's blows." She shuddered.

Eliza, who had at first expected a billet-doux, unfolded the paper with relief and read aloud, " 'Take

142

one ounce of butter without salt, one-half ounce of white wax, two drachmas of prepared tutty, a scruple of camphire, one tablespoon of rosewater. Let all this simmer a few minutes and stir it till cold. Bind it over the eyes before going to bed and wash the next morning with tutty and elderflower water.' It does sound salubrious."

"Oh, it is. My old nurse swore by it. Actually, May butter is best, but there's no help for that. He must simply make do. The thing is, Miss Osborne, I'm very desirous that Mr. Slaughter should have access to this remedy. But it would never do to ask one of Lady Wenham's servants to deliver it."

"No, I expect not," Eliza concurred.

"But no one would think twice about a charitable gesture originating from the vicarage. So would it be too much to ask you to see that Mr. Slaughter receives this?"

"Not at all." Eliza was feeling a bit noble herself. "And I'll certainly see that Mr. Slaughter learns the source of it."

Lady Juliet went pink again. "Oh, but that's not at all necessary."

"On, but I collect it is. For I'm convinced that the source of the recipe will be the ointment's most curative property."

Lady Juliet soon took her leave and Eliza carried the paper into the kitchen, where, under Betty's disapproving eye, she prepared the mixture herself. "You're certainly full of good works, miss," the servant said with a sniff. "I just hope you ain't thinking of delivering that mess yourself, but just in case you are that rackety, please don't tell me about it so I can remain in honest ignorance if Mrs. Tomkins should ask me where you've gone."

Chapter
Seventeen

"*Oh, my goodness, you do look dreadful. Jervis* was right. You actually look worse than you did yesterday, and I had not thought it possible."

Eliza had been waiting for some time in Mr. Slaughter's drawing room, a chamber more comfortable than elegant, with its well-worn furniture and lack of feminine adornment. On his entrance she had jumped up from her chair in consternation. Now she stared in horror at his battered face, colorfully streaked with blacks and blues and highlighted with liverish-looking slits. "Oh, I was wrong in coming. I've caused you to get out of bed."

"Some Job's comforter you are," he retorted thickly. "I recognize the fact that I'm no beauty, but I hadn't expected to turn you into stone. I heartily agree with what you said, though. You were wrong in coming here. But not because you got me out of bed. You didn't. You'll no doubt be pleased to hear that I don't feel as bad as I look."

"Thank God for that," she said fervently.

He laughed, then winced at the pain it cost him. "I'll vow I didn't feel half bad till I had to stand here and watch your stomach turn at the sight of me. I hope you realize that as a ministering angel you leave a lot to be desired. At least I collect you're on a mercy mission. What *is* that you're clutching?" He nodded at the jar she was clasping in both hands. "If it's medicinal, perhaps you should take it. You certainly look a lot more ill than I'm feeling at the moment."

"Oh, this." She'd forgotten all about the salve, but now she thrust it toward him. "You don't *take* it, you smear it on. It's an ointment for your eyes."

"Well, thank you very much." He removed the jar lid and sniffed its contents doubtfully.

"Oh, it's not from me. Well, I did concoct it. But the recipe is Lady Juliet's. She heard that you were hurt, you see, and was terribly upset by it. Couldn't sleep in fact, she told me."

"Indeed?" The voice was noncommittal, and though Eliza tried, it was impossible to read his feelings in his battered face.

"She says it's most efficacious. The remedy's been in her family for years. Though I can't imagine why, for it's difficult to picture any of Lady Juliet's kin in your condition."

"Ouch! For God's sake, don't make me laugh. It plays the devil with this lip."

"Oh, I am sorry. But I wasn't aware I was saying anything amusing."

"That's because you haven't met her father. A more stiff-rumped, platter-faced mortal isn't imaginable. It was the thought of him stripping and climbing into the ring that did it."

"Well, in that respect, he sounds most sensible.

For of all the mutton-headed, bird-witted, altogether insane things to do, boxing has to be—"

"No! Stop! Just hold it right there if you please, Miss Osborne. I fully intend to ring a peal over you, and I'm not going to be diverted by you flinging my follies in my face."

"Believe me, I'd not dream of flinging anything in your face. It's had all that it can bear. I would not be so cruel."

"Never mind my face." He stood glaring down at her. "What I wish to say is, a lady like you should never have gone to that mill. It simply isn't done. And when I'm more myself I'm damned if I won't flatten Jervis for taking you."

"Oh, don't do that, for heaven's sake. He certainly didn't want to."

"Well, then, he'd no business letting you bear-lead him. Just because he's been henpecked from the cradle by that mother of his doesn't mean he has to knuckle under to anyone in skirts.

"But never mind Jervis, either. You're the case at issue here. And I'm deuced if I can figure you out at all, Eliza. I've rarely met anyone who seems so genuinely proper but who still insists on acting in the most improper ways. Do you know that your father has my deepest sympathy? You must have driven the poor man to bedlam in your—what is it, nineteen?—years."

"No, that's what I did not do," she responded seriously as she walked over to a couch and sat down on it.

"Do make yourself at home," he said dryly, then shrugged and sat beside her.

She was too engrossed in analyzing her own actions to notice his reluctant hospitality. "My improper conduct, as you call it, seemed to start with my decision to come to Claxton without Papa's knowledge. Once I'd acted quite independently, everything else just seemed to follow. But I see no need for you to concern yourself. After I return home I shall no doubt revert to my old habits. My independence is probably just brought on by the Sussex air."

"Well, I must say that preaching propriety is a new role for me. But believe me, Eliza, I would hate to see your character come to harm from our association. I value your friendship too much to tarnish your reputation. Gossip travels fast. Believe me, for I speak with authority. It can cover the distance between here and your home with lightning speed."

"Really, it's not necessary for you to prose on and on," she said crossly. "You've made your point."

"Have I? Somehow I doubt it. Your problem, Eliza, is that for all your recent rackety behavior, you're an innocent."

"And for an ex-rake, ex-convict, and ex-pugilist, you certainly have a penchant for preaching. Why don't you just borrow my uncle's pulpit and be done with it?"

"My, my, we are waspish, aren't we? Well, no doubt I should beg your pardon for the lecture. Especially after you were so kind as to bring me this . . . stuff." He set the jar he'd been holding down on the sofa table. "But I'm damned if I'm going to. Because for some strange reason, ever since I saw you sidling toward Gentleman Jack in the coach yard, I've felt responsible for you."

"Fustian."

"No, it's true. Ridiculous, I grant you, but true. And now that I've placed myself *in loco parentis*, so to speak, why don't you go on and tell me what's put you into such a taking."

"I'm not in a taking. Or if I am, it could be because I thought I was doing you a kindness by delivering Lady Juliet's ointment this way. And I did not expect to be scolded for it. In point of fact, I rather expected you'd go into raptures," Eliza told him.

"Raptures? You really have a lot more faith in this concoction than I have. Is it some miracle cure?"

"You know perfectly well what I mean. I thought you'd be in rap—*pleased* by her concern."

"Oh, I am."

Once again it was impossible for Eliza to read his face. But even so, her spirits sank another notch, which rather surprised her since she could have sworn they'd hit rock bottom with Lady Juliet's concern for the battered man beside her.

Garrick changed the subject. "You've never told me, you know, just why you set out alone that day."

"Oh, did I not?" She was glad to redirect her thoughts. "My father had just remarried, you see, and was due home from his honeymoon. I felt I would be in the way."

"Hmmmm." His eyes, even narrowed as they were by the swelling, seemed to look right through her. "And is that all?"

"Isn't it enough?"

"I suppose so. Only I seem to be learning to read your mind."

She looked up at him in a state of alarm, fervently hoping it wasn't so.

"And I think what we have here is a half-truth," he mused. "Oh, what you've just said supplies a good enough reason for you to plan a visit to your aunt. But it's hardly sufficient to put you into flight. Would you care to tell me the rest of it?"

After a little more prodding on his part, Eliza found herself pouring out the story of her father's matchmaking and of how she'd nipped his marriage plans for her in the bud, then fled rather than face his displeasure and disappointment. "It was quite craven of me," she concluded.

"But prudent, perhaps. Your instincts were possibly right. It won't hurt to give your father time to cool. He'll surely realize the folly of wedding you to a man like that."

"That's just what he won't do." Her chin quivered as she told him of Sir Charles's letter. "He's expecting me to change my mind, you see." And to her horror and chagrin, tears began to gather in her eyes. Whether this humiliating condition was caused by her own bleak matrimonial prospects or from having been the bearer of Lady Juliet's token of affection to the man beside her, she couldn't say.

But it was quite evident that the gathering tears alarmed Garrick Slaughter almost as much as they mortified her.

"I say, you mustn't do that. This isn't at all like you, Eliza." He threw a protective arm around her shoulders and gave her a little shake. "Come on, where's your fighting spirit, child? You can stand up to your father. He's not some ogre who'll marry you against your wishes, now is he?"

"N-no. Oh, blast!" The tears were coming fast in spite of everything. She wanted to sink. "I think I'd best be going."

"No! Not while you're imitating a curst rainstorm. Here." Garrick fished in a pocket to produce a handkerchief and began to dab at her eyes and cheeks. "This is rather like trying to blot up the Thames."

She giggled, albeit snuffily.

"Ah, that's better. That's my girl." After a few more dabs, he appraised his work, then planted a light kiss on her forehead. It was perhaps unfortunate that she reacted by raising her face in some astonishment, for if he'd meant to repeat the brotherly performance, it went awry. His swollen lips met her parted ones solidly and there was nothing in what followed that suggested a chaste kinship of any kind. When he finally wrenched himself away, he was breathing almost as heavily as he had at the conclusion of his mill.

He collapsed back against the sofa arm and touched his mouth gingerly, while Eliza stared at him, her face shuttered. "Gad, that was painful."

"Yes, it was," she replied softly as she rose to her feet, smoothing down her rumpled walking dress.

He rose, too. "Dammit, I've done it again, haven't I? I don't seem to learn. I'm sorry, Eliza. I truly am. It was despicable of me to take advantage of the circumstances."

"Oh, please. Don't go through all that again. You've already preached propriety to me. Let's just call this one more object lesson."

"Let's do nothing of the sort. What do you take me for? I'd rather be thought a cad than a hypocrite. I kissed you because I couldn't help myself, not to teach you anything. But I had no right to take advantage of your being here alone. Or of the fact that you're distressed over being pressured to marry the widower. God knows I'd whisk you to the altar myself if I didn't realize you'd be far, far better off with a clodpole like him than with an alumnus of Newgate."

"Don't be a ninnyhammer," she snapped. "Newgate or no Newgate, there's no need to blow a mere kiss out of all proportion."

"A *mere* kiss?" Given his distorted features it was hard to tell, but she thought he looked offended. "Oh, I'll grant you, our behavior was not proper, but I suspect you've confused some of the actual pain that you were feeling for passion. I, for one, did not find the experience extraordinary enough to account for the Cheltenham tragedy you're making of it."

"I'm doing no such thing. I simply wish to make it clear that—"

"I know," Eliza interrupted with a fling of her head. "You want me to know that you would nobly sacrifice yourself and marry me were you not living underneath the cloud of disgrace. Do you realize that there's a strong streak of martyrdom in your family? Your brother recently expressed much the same sentiment. And it would not amaze me to learn that your father spoke somewhat along those same lines to your mother."

"Go to the devil, Eliza."

"And you go smear some of this ... glop upon your face." She snatched up the jar of ointment and hurled it at him. He managed to catch it before it reached its target, but winced at the impact in his hand.

"Vixen!"

"Martyr!"

She spat the word back over her shoulder as she hurried from the room. She added emphasis by slamming the door behind her.

Chapter
Eighteen

Eliza had thought it impossible to feel any worse. She had just made a complete cake of herself. It was now useless to imagine that Garrick Slaughter didn't know she was in love with him, a condition she'd been at some pains to hide, even from herself. She railed at herself all the way back to the vicarage for her behavior, starting at the point when she'd decided to deliver Lady Juliet Greenwood's elixir personally, a piece of martyrdom she ranked right up there with Garrick's hypocritical marriage offer. She went sneaking into the vicarage, hoping to reach the sanctuary of her room and lick her wounds in peace. She was sure that the day and her life had hit rock bottom. She was wrong.

"Oh, there you are, m'dear," Aunt Hester called with false brightness as Eliza walked softly past the open drawing-room door.

"We'd almost despaired of you," Uncle George

chimed in. "Where could you have been all this time?"

Oh, heavens, she was trapped. And to make matters even worse, her aunt and uncle were entertaining a visitor. It was only when that visitor turned her way that the full damage of the day was reckoned. Eliza stared, transfixed, at the middle-aged, middle-sized gentleman whose fair hair was beginning to thin as his waistline started to bulge and whose protuberant blue eyes were watching her rather warily. "Mr. Cox!" she gasped, her face and voice appalled.

"Yes, is it not delightful?" Mrs. Tomkins made a valiant effort to cover her niece's dismay. "Mr. Cox is on his way to Brighton. He's broken his journey particularly to see us."

"Don't just stand there, m'dear," the Reverend Tomkins chided. "Do come in and join us. We've been waiting our tea for you."

After a few words of greeting during which Eliza tried to make up for her incivility with inquiries about the health of the visitor's children, his sister, and her father, followed by an interlude when Mrs. Tomkins poured out the tea and saw to it that their guest was amply supplied with ginger nuts and bread and butter, Mr. Cox turned to Eliza.

"I've brought a letter to you, Miss Osborne, from your father. And I was just sharing with your aunt and uncle what I believe to be the tenor of his message. When your father learned that I must come this way on business, you see, he requested that I stop by here and fetch you back home in my carriage."

"Oh, dear."

Again, Mrs. Tomkins tried to compensate. "I've been telling Mr. Cox"—her smile was forced—"that it is much, much too soon for you to end your visit. He says, though, that your father is adamant, as his letter will doubtlessly reveal. But Mr. Cox has

153

kindly agreed to postpone his journey home until after Mr. Wenham's coming-of-age ball."

"Yes," Mr. Cox condescended, "I can see that it would be a crushing tragedy to keep you from such a treat, Miss Osborne. I myself caught a glimpse of the Hall as I drove in, and I must say it is magnificent. Your father will understand the delay when I explain that I could not be so cruel as to tear you away before that social occasion."

"And I've been trying to persuade Mr. Cox to attend the ball," the vicar chimed in. "For I'm sure that once it's known we have a guest, he will most certainly be included in our invitation." He stopped short, rendered speechless by an uncharacteristic glare from his dear helpmeet.

But Mr. Cox, who, fortunately, had been looking at Eliza, hastened to explain that he'd brought no evening clothes. Besides, he was not at all partial to dancing. No, he'd simply remain in Brighton another day or so. The press of his business would probably make this new arrangement advantageous.

The vicar, bewildered by the currents swirling all around him, still tried to play the gracious host. "At least," he said, a bit too brightly, "Mr. Cox has generously consented to delay his business plans and spend some time with us. I've convinced him that he must see our lovely countryside."

On the following day, the only silver lining to the cloud that hovered over Eliza's life was that at least the gentleman avoided the subject of marriage. True, he was given little opportunity to raise it, for Mrs. Tomkins seemed bent upon helping her niece entertain him. Without a word having been spoken, she picked up on Eliza's appeal and showed Mr. Cox an excessive attention that could almost have been construed as chaperonage.

But rather than being put out of countenance by

154

her aunt's presence, Mr. Cox appeared to deem it an advantage. Of a naturally garrulous disposition, he occupied their time together by acquainting Mrs. Tomkins with his standing in the business community he came from. Whether this was intended simply to impress her aunt with his consequence or to make Eliza regret the folly of turning down his offer of marriage and thereby soften her up for the next proposal, that young lady was at a loss to say. She did, however, fear the worst.

They exhausted the best walks on the first day of his visit. It was the vicar who suggested the following morning at breakfast that Mr. Cox might like to see the abbey ruins. At first the visitor appeared lukewarm toward the proffered treat, but when Mrs. Tomkins regretted that parish duties made it impossible for her to join the lengthy expedition, he became all eagerness.

His enthusiasm waned a bit, though, when he saw the donkey cart. "Since we'll need to leave the road, it's the most practical means of transportation," Eliza explained. "Besides, we couldn't see the countryside nearly so well in the closed carriage." She neglected to say that the coachman was also the gardener, or vice versa, and it would not do to take him from his duties.

Mr. Cox eyed the animals with obvious distaste. And he did not demur when Eliza elected to drive the little cart herself. "Pity I chose to travel in a hired post chaise," he said, sighing. "No doubt you wish I had my own rig now."

"Which one?" she dutifully inquired. Mr. Cox had managed to bring into the conversation more than once that he kept two carriages.

"Well, now, that does present a problem." He warmed to a favorite subject. "The traveling coach would be totally impractical right now, whereas the gig would never have done for my long journey. I'm thinking seriously of acquiring a third." He tried unsuccessfully to sound offhand as the small cart bumped its way along. "Your father thinks it a needless extravagance. But I say that a little extravagance now and again is not totally to be despised. Tell me, Miss Osborne, what would you say to a landaulet?"

What Eliza would have liked to say was that she didn't care a fig what kind of carriage he bought, but that if he truly wanted her opinion she considered landaulets much too dowdy for words. She was fortunately saved the necessity of replying since at that moment the donkeys decided to balk.

"What the devil's the matter with them?"

"It's the bridge." She sighed. "They don't like it. And about one time out of every three they simply refuse to cross it. Unfortunately, this seems to be one of those times." She handed him the reins and climbed out of the cart.

"What are you doing, Miss Osborne?" Mr. Cox could not have looked more alarmed if she'd abandoned ship.

"Sometimes you can lead them across." She sounded doubtful even to herself.

At the best of times the donkeys were not notable for cooperation, and this, obviously, was to be one of their more trying days. Eliza began with soft-voiced cajoling, a technique made even more difficult under Mr. Cox's critical eye. Just as she hoped to have instilled a bit of confidence and was all set to tug upon the reins, he barked impatiently, "Oh, really, Miss Osborne, your conversation is absurd. They are only dumb beasts and should be treated so." This explosion effectively broke into any spell she might have woven, and when she did pull on the bridles, the donkeys merely rolled their eyes in protest and dug their little hooves in all the harder.

"Someone's coming and we're blocking the bridge," Mr. Cox called out.

Oh, dear. Sure enough, history was now repeating itself, with only the slightest variation. Mr. Wenham and Mr. Slaughter were both on horseback this time as they came around the bend, and Lady Juliet was not with them.

"Stand aside!" Mr. Cox ordered, and she did so. He rose to his feet, picked up the whip, and began to ply it furiously, lashing the donkeys with all the force at his command.

"Stop it!" Eliza screamed, while at the same time the donkeys reared and kicked, pulling in different directions in order to dodge the blows. The cart rocked precariously, this way and that, and Mr. Cox went tumbling over the side. Now freed of their persecutor, the donkeys pulled in concert and dashed with the empty cart across the bridge.

Eliza had wheeled upon Mr. Cox, who was picking himself up out of the ditch, and was giving him a furious tongue-lashing when Mr. Wenham and Mr. Slaughter came dashing up. "That was a brutish thing to do!" she concluded.

"Still in a temper, Miss Osborne? Aren't you even going to ask the gentleman how he is?" Mr. Slaughter inquired while Mr. Wenham remarked, *sotto voce*, that it would serve the gentleman right if he'd broken his damned neck.

Mr. Cox was brushing himself off and looking thunderous. It was obvious that his dignity, if not his body, had been done a fearful injury. "You fail to understand, sir," he spoke stiffly to Mr. Wenham, "that this was the only way to shift the beasts. All else failed. We could have been here the rest of the day if I hadn't used the whip on 'em."

"Well, yes," Mr. Slaughter observed, "I can see that you've certainly solved the problem."

Mr. Cox moved one step closer to apoplexy.

"Are you all right, sir?" Eliza made a supreme effort to sound civil that almost achieved its goal. When he mumbled that he thought so, she continued in the same overly polite tone, "Then may I present the Honorable Jervis Wenham and Mr. Slaughter. And this is Mr. Cox, who is brother to my father's wife."

"I rather thought so," Mr. Slaughter said as the gentlemen nodded with little enthusiasm at one another. Mr. Cox appeared even more put out by the discovery that he'd taken his undignified tumble in the presence of the heir to Warleigh Hall. Mr. Slaughter's remark, however, focused his attention there, and his eyes widened.

His obvious astonishment called for enlightenment. "Mr. Slaughter is a pugilist," Eliza said, instinctively trying to avoid Garrick's eyes and suppress the memory of their most recent meeting. "He has just defeated Savage Stenhouse in a mill."

"I'll wager you're wondering what the Savage looks like." Jervis snickered.

Eliza steeled herself then to study Garrick's face. Although it was even more colorful than before, with some yellows added to the blacks and blues, at least the swelling was going down. She was relieved to see that his nose promised to return to its previous proportions. "Actually, he looks very much improved," was her spoken verdict. "The salve that Lady—that is to say, that *I* . . . that my aunt's maid, actually—prepared for him must really be remarkable."

"Quite," Garrick commented briefly, while Jervis gave him a puzzled look. "Now why don't I go see if I can round up your donkeys. Surely they're winded by now." With a tip of his hat toward Eliza and a nod for Mr. Cox, he cantered away.

"Pray don't let us detain you, Mr. Wenham," Eliza said pointedly after they'd watched Garrick ride out of sight. But Jervis had dismounted and seemed in no hurry to be off. He was engaging Mr. Cox in a conversation that appeared to be mollifying that gentleman's injured feelings but sounded to Eliza's ears very much like an inquisition.

But since Mr. Cox's favorite topic of conversation was himself, he was not at all reluctant to reveal his background and aspirations. When he confided to this stranger that he'd been a widower for well over a year now and felt it incumbent upon himself to provide a mother for his orphaned children, Eliza was ready to sink and could not bring herself to look at Jervis Wenham.

"Very sensible of you, sir," that gentleman replied. "And I'm sure you'll be sensible enough to choose a wife of mature years. It's wonderful how often widowers make the mistake of marrying females very little older than their children. And with disastrous results. But I can tell that you, sir, are a man of sense and wouldn't make that kind of error."

Mr. Cox's feathers were ruffling once again; Eliza deemed it time to change the subject. "Oh, Mr. Wenham. Mr. Cox is thinking of purchasing a third carriage. Perhaps you can advise him."

At first her choice of topic seemed fortuitous, for Mr. Cox brightened considerably. But Jervis soon grew Friday-faced at the mere mention of the word *landaulet*. It was therefore providential that Garrick Slaughter was seen approaching, driving the donkey cart with his stallion tethered behind it.

After an awkward word of thanks, they took their leave. Eliza and Mr. Cox walked back to the vicarage, with her leading the donkeys. (He'd stiffly declined to go and visit the abbey ruins; he'd also refused to climb into the cart.) When she finally found the leisure, if not the inclination, to look back over the disastrous day, its only saving grace was that Mr. Cox had not had the opportunity to renew his offer of marriage, which she was sure he'd planned to do at the romantic ruins.

An even more cheerful thought was that perhaps he'd lost the inclination. Certainly he'd been out of charity with her over the entire donkey episode.

Nor did he approve of her choice of friends. He had remarked pointedly that he could not imagine how she'd ever come to be acquainted with a pugilist. And as for Mr. Wenham, well, he'd appeared too toplofty by half for Mr. Cox's taste. Even so, Eliza nourished the hope that Jervis's none-too-subtle words about an older wife might have taken root and would flourish in Mr. Cox's mind.

That hope was dashed the next morning when Mr. Cox took his leave of them. For even as her aunt and uncle hovered dutifully in the background, he managed to whisper over Eliza's hand, "I'm looking forward to our trip home together, Miss Osborne. For I intend to reintroduce a topic that I know has been foremost in both our minds. And I do hope that this time you will not feel it necessary to your consequence to keep me dangling any longer." Then, after a squeeze of her hand and a significant look, he hurried down the path to the waiting post chaise.

"Mr. Cox seems a most substantial gentleman, Eliza," Mr. Tomkins remarked as the coach disappeared from sight and the three of them turned to go back indoors. "You are most fortunate to have fixed his interest."

"Rubbish!" Mrs. Tomkins proclaimed in a ringing tone that caused her saintly spouse to gape in astonishment.

Chapter Nineteen

"*There's going to be an announcement tonight.*" Lady Cheselden leaned across the dining table to confide this bit of information to Eliza in a carrying tone that riveted the attention of every guest in the immediate vicinity.

Eliza smiled—noncommittally, she hoped. She also hoped it was not too obvious that she was developing a headache.

Really, it was too absurd. Here she was, attending the social occasion that should have been the highlight of her visit—indeed, her life—and she was finding it tedious in the extreme. It had been just her luck, or Lady Wenham's design more likely, to be placed opposite the dowager whose very presence precluded any hope of general conversation. And it had not helped matters to look far down the mahogany table and see Lady Juliet, ravishing in a British net frock over blue satin, and Jervis, looking heartbreakingly handsome in his stark black and white evening clothes, gazing into one another's eyes. Now, the knowledge that those two were about to become officially betrothed was the last straw needed to plunge her down into the dismals. Or perhaps, in truth, neither of those things had all that much to say in the matter. Tomorrow and Mr. Cox were the real culprits.

"You don't look up to snuff, Miss Osborne." Lady Cheselden's latest remark caused all heads within hearing to turn and stare curiously at Eliza. "Been trying to decide why and at last I've got it. You should have worn a necklace." She stared critically at Eliza's white crape round dress that was cut low to her bosom. "Don't you have any jewels, child?"

"Not with me." Eliza tried to speak repressively.

The attempt was futile. "Well, never you mind," the other replied condescendingly. "I've the very thing in my jewel box. You can borrow it for the evening."

Much to Eliza's relief, the gentleman seated next to her ladyship interposed a question and she was set off once more upon a different tack. Eliza took a forkful of oyster collops and allowed her thoughts to wander.

Lady Cheselden's talk of jewelry had inevitably made her mind revert to the stolen diamonds. It was hard now to credit that she'd been naïve enough to believe that eventually the truth would out and Garrick Slaughter would be exonerated. She was no nearer to knowing who the culprit was than when she'd first arrived.

No, she corrected herself, that was not quite accurate. She did know who the people were who'd been in the London town house on that dreadful night and had had the opportunity to slip a pair of earrings into the greatcoat pocket of a castaway young man. And she had an inkling of the truth. It was proof that remained elusive.

She gazed around her, focusing, one at a time, on the members of the Wenham household who could have done such a wicked thing. It was almost inconceivable that one of these sophisticated people, dressed in evening finery, dining on the finest china underneath the glow of an enormous crystal chandelier, could have maliciously sent an innocent man to prison. Could any of these well-bred faces conceal a secret as despicable as that?

Far up the table in the seat of honor, Jervis was gazing at Lady Juliet, who was talking to the gentleman on her other side. His expression contrived somehow to look both miserable and adoring. In the beginning he had been Eliza's number-one suspect. He'd had ample reason to be jealous of his brother and the most to gain by ruining him. But Eliza no longer considered Jervis a possibility. There was nothing feigned about his love for Garrick Slaughter. Besides, she now knew him incapable of such a deed.

Her eyes moved on to the head of the table and rested on Lord Wenham: distinguished, handsome, the perfect host. He, of course, had never actually been a suspect. The only mystery about him, she thought, was how this pattern card of respectability had ever fallen head over heels for a woman so far beneath his touch and fathered a child by her. For there was no doubt but that his affair with Garrick's mother had been far more than the usual wild-oats sowing of his class. His treatment of his illegitimate offspring testified to that. As did Lady Wenham's jealousy.

Eliza's glance whisked past Lady Cheselden, afraid to pause there and be sucked into a conversation. But the old lady had been in the town house on that fateful night, and who knew whether or not she'd had a sudden impulse to look after her grandson's interests. Granted, it was difficult to think of her looking after anyone else's interests but her own. Still . . .

And there'd been another "harmless" old lady present when the jewels were taken, Eliza recalled. She scanned the thirty or so diners till she located Miss Hurst, seated even farther "below the salt" than she was.

The lady's face was flushed and her purple turban sat slightly askew, the results, Eliza observed, of an overeager consumption of the wines that the alert footmen kept replenishing. What a life the woman must have led, she thought with a rush of pity. Miss Hurst was the proverbial poor relation, brought into the household as an act of charity: first, to look after little Jervis, and, when that necessity was done with, passed on to run and fetch for an impossible old lady. Would it be any wonder if the old maid's affections had become so centered on the child she'd cared for that she'd lose all sense of right and wrong where his interests were concerned?

And, of course, one should never forget the servants. Not these in the Hall, but the ones in London. Perhaps some maid or footman had taken the jewels and then, fearing discovery, had quickly disposed of them, not intending malice but just meaning to go to Garrick's rooms later on . . . Oh, really, that was far too fanciful!

Eliza had saved Lady Wenham for last. She now turned her attention toward the foot of the table where her ladyship, resplendent in rubies and a ruby-colored turban, was smiling at her dinner partner's anecdote, while at the same time allowing her eyes to stray above the row of silver candelabra toward the head of the table where her husband sat.

Eliza's review of the other suspects had been mere academic exercise. There was no doubt in her mind that Lady Wenham had deliberately incriminated her husband's love child. And she was also certain that both Lord Wenham and his legitimate son strongly suspected the same thing. And as for Garrick Slaughter, she'd wager all she owned that he was convinced of it.

But there was no proof that her ladyship had done so, and there never would be. Even on the off chance that one of the servants had seen her with her hand in Garrick's greatcoat pocket, who would be brave enough to risk dismissal by saying so? Even more to the point, who would take a servant's word above Lady Wenham's?

Eliza sat and toyed with her food and at the same time toyed with the notion of taking her ladyship aside during the course of the evening and dramatically hurling this accusation in her face: I know that you put your own diamonds in Mr. Slaughter's pocket, so confess, you villainess!

Well, that might work in some of the more far-fetched, horrid gothic novels, but she could well imagine the look of contempt it would elicit from Lady Wenham.

No, Eliza reflected gloomily, her ladyship would carry her guilty secret to the grave. Just as Garrick Slaughter would carry the crime's stigma. As for herself, she'd go away leaving the mystery unsolved, never to see any of those involved again.

"Miss Osborne!" Lady Cheselden's bark snapped Eliza out of her reverie. "You've scarce said a word all evening. Not since I told you there'd be an announcement later. Well, there's no use having a fit of the sulks because my grandson's about to become betrothed. Didn't I tell you from the start not to go setting your cap for him? He's far above your touch. That's what I told you."

Eliza's face flamed scarlet once again. This time all of the diners within earshot studiously avoided looking in her direction. She fought down the urge to pick up a bowl of cauliflower ragout and fling it at the odious old dragon's head. Instead, she turned her attention to the gentleman on her right. "My uncle tells me that you and he were at school together." This worthy rose to the occasion and obliged with a long, drawn-out account of his and the vicar's schooldays that carried them, mercifully, through the final course.

At the conclusion of the meal, Eliza was unable to dodge Lady Cheselden and so resigned herself to wearing whatever necklace the old woman had in mind rather than making a scene by arguing the point. No doubt it would be enormous and garish, to set off her ladyship's personality.

She was therefore agreeably surprised when her ladyship selected a single strand of pearls hung with a sapphire pendant from the jewelry box her maid had fetched. It was perfect, Eliza concluded, as she admired the effect in the cheval glass.

"That's better," her ladyship pronounced, dismissing her maid to return the box to its place of concealment. "Maybe now you'll attract some young squire who'll mistake you for an heiress."

"I'm not penniless, you know," Eliza was stung into replying as she turned away from the glass. "And why you should persist in thinking . . ." She completely forgot what she'd meant to say as her eyes focused on Lady Cheselden.

The dowager was seated at her dressing table securing the second of a pair of diamond eardrops in her ear. The jewelry was magnificent. A large, teardrop diamond dangled from a row of smaller stones and danced with sparkles in the candlelight. Eliza gaped at the earrings, doubting the testimony of her own eyes. She'd heard the jewelry described often enough, but still . . . "Surely those aren't . . . They can't be . . ." she blurted out.

"The eardrops that caused all the fuss?" The old lady chuckled wickedly. "Of course they are."

"But you surely don't intend to wear them!"

"Of course I do!" She glared at Eliza's reflection in the glass. "I'm eighty-four years old, missy. Just how many grand occasions do you think will come along for me?"

"But don't you consider it, well, to say the least, tactless?"

"Not a bit of it! Oh, I didn't wear 'em down to dinner where Wenham just might have noticed. But he's not going to spare a glance for me in the crush there'll be downstairs. And as for Jervis, who's the only other person who might be upset if he saw these beauties"—she turned her head from side to side to get the full effect of all the dazzle in the glass—"well, he'll not take his eyes off that gorgeous girl all night. As you're bound to realize, to your sorrow."

"But still, how can you?"

"How can I?" Lady Cheselden's voice cracked in indignation. "I'll have you know, Miss Osborne, that by rights these beauties should have belonged to me. They've been in my late husband's family for generations and were always handed down to the bride of the eldest son. But Cheselden's old witch of a mother hung on to them like glue, then passed them on to Charlotte at her come-out just to spite me. We couldn't abide one another from the outset, don't you see. And in this instance Cheselden took her part, said the stones were hers to do with as she pleased. Well, they weren't! By rights they should have come to me. It was *tradition.* And she broke it. These eardrops were mine! To dispose of as I wished. Oh, but I got my own back all right. And killed two birds with one stone, you might say."

All of a sudden, Eliza forgot to breathe. She felt sick and giddy. Lady Cheselden's face was blurring in the glass, obscured, or so it seemed, by the increased dazzle of the diamonds. But when she was finally able to find her voice, it sounded amazingly calm, almost detached, as if the words were being uttered by someone else. "Are you saying, Lady Cheselden, that it was you who put the diamonds in Garrick Slaughter's pocket?"

For just a moment a look of protective cunning dominated the wrinkled face. But its expression changed quickly to belligerence. "They were mine, I tell you. I could do whatever I wanted with them."

"Including sending an innocent man to prison?"

"Innocent!" Lady Cheselden swung around on the dressing-table bench to confront Eliza directly. "Innocent! How dare you use such a term to describe that bastard! There's nothing *innocent* about cheating my grandson out of his inheritance. There's nothing *innocent* in the way he tried to overset Jervis in his father's affections. And then, to have the slut's son come marching into my own daughter's house as if he had every right to be there—well, I can tell you, missy, that was the outside of enough! Oh, yes, I fixed his nibs good and proper. It was a stroke of brilliance, if I do say so myself. Especially since Charlotte didn't want to wear these earrings ever again and said I might keep them. But enough of all that. I need to get downstairs to my grandson's party."

Lady Charlotte faced the glass once more to give her turban a final adjustment. "Pity I didn't have these diamonds while I was still a beauty and could do 'em justice." She gave the ruins of her face a dissatisfied scowl. "Still"—she cheered up just as quickly—"no schoolroom miss could hope to carry 'em off. It takes an air of consequence. And no one can deny me that. Well, we'd best get down to the ball, Miss Osborne, if you're to have any hopes of snaring a beau. Why, what do you think you're doing?"

Eliza was unclasping the strand of pearls and removing them from her throat. "Here." She placed the necklace upon the dressing table. "Just don't go sticking this in some poor culprit's pocket, you wicked old woman!" She hurried across the room.

"If you tell anyone what I've just said I'll deny it!" Lady Cheselden's screech was answered by a slamming door.

Eliza was forced to wait until Lord and Lady Wenham had received their guests and officially opened the ball before she could seek out his lordship and whisper that she must speak to him on a matter of great urgency. Then they closeted themselves in his library while she poured out her story. At the conclusion of it his lordship's face was a mixture of horror, disgust, and relief. "What a fool I was not to have realized. But there seemed no doubt at first. And then later on I feared . . ." He clamped his lips tight against what he might have said, and Eliza tactfully appeared not to notice.

"Lady Cheselden will deny all this, your lordship."

His face set grimly. "Never mind that. I'll make sure that the truth becomes known."

Eliza left him then to go in search of Mrs. Tomkins. She spied her aunt seated with a group of other matrons who were watching the sets perform a country dance. As she hurried toward them, she saw Lord Wenham enter the ballroom and draw his son aside. After a whispered consultation, the two men left together.

Eliza sat down beside her aunt and spoke low enough for no one else to hear. "I'm going home now, Aunt Hester. Please don't ask me to explain why, but I must go. And no, don't you come, too. It will look peculiar. I wish to slip out unnoticed."

It took a bit more convincing and several assurances that, no, she wasn't ill, before her aunt, though looking most distressed, finally agreed.

As Eliza hurried down the carriage drive, music from the orchestra drifted behind her. Just before she reached the curve where the trees would shield it from her sight, she turned for one last look at Warleigh Hall. This was the way she'd like to remember it: bathed and softened by the moonlight, its windows ablaze, while music and the muted sounds of revelry were carried on the soft night breeze. No need to think of the sordid drama being played out inside the ivy-covered walls. All that was no longer any concern of hers.

The thought was not nearly as uplifting as it should have been. She squinted hard at the manor house, trying to commit every detail to memory. Blast Jervis anyhow! If he hadn't destroyed her sketch so cavalierly, she'd have no need for all this mental exertion.

Somehow, being out of charity with Jervis once again was rather comforting. She turned her back on Warleigh Hall, hitched up her skirts, and began to run toward the vicarage.

Chapter
Twenty

*E*liza *was relieved to find that Betty had gone to* bed. She regretted though that the maid had already packed her belongings for tomorrow's journey. She'd looked forward to doing that herself to occupy her spinning mind.

Instead, she brewed a cup of tea and settled down in the drawing room to drink it. There, she gave her mind full rein. Perhaps the sooner she could deal with all that had happened and put her adventures since leaving home to rest, the better off she'd be.

The odd thing was, she felt no elation. Scarcely two hours before she had sat at dinner bemoaning the fact that no one would ever know how the earrings came to be in Garrick Slaughter's pocket. Now she had solved the mystery. And she should be rejoicing over that instead of sitting here, giving in to a dismal attack of the blue-devils. Could it be that in her heart of hearts she'd hoped that if Garrick remained disgraced he might eventually turn to her by default?

No, indeed! she defended herself stoutly. Until this very moment such a thought had never entered her mind. And once the shock of events had worn off and she was herself again, she was positive she could wish Garrick every happiness, although—

"Eliza! Hurry up and get your things together," commanded a low voice from the doorway.

"Eek!" She jumped sky-high. Tea sloshed out of the cup onto her ball gown. "Now see what you've made me do, Jervis! What's the meaning of sneaking up on a—"

"Shhh!" He strode across the room to clap his hand upon her mouth. "Do you want to wake the household?"

She angrily pushed the hand away but did oblige him by dropping her voice to whisper-level. "You scared me out of my wits, you ninny. What do you mean by sneaking up on me like that?"

"You're the ninny. You don't go hammering on the door and have yourself admitted for an elopement. I saw you through the window and—"

"An elopement!"

The hand flew back into place. "There you go again. I never knew such a female for screeching. Now when I take my hand away this time I want you to tiptoe *quietly* and get some things together. You and I are going to Gretna Green."

"You're insane," she whispered when the white glove was once more removed. "Stark, raving mad. We can't possibly go to Gretna Green."

"We can if you get into action. But if we simply stand round here arguing the point, someone's sure to come. For God's sake, Eliza, just go get your things. And don't bother to change, either. I'll explain everything on the way."

"I'm not going anywhere with you. Besides every
172

other consideration, you're betrothed. You're going to marry Lady Juliet."

"No I'm not. Garrick is."

"Oh." That was a leveler.

"At least he will be if we manage to give him the opportunity. He's just now learning that his name's been cleared, don't you see. So I had to get away before they made that curst announcement. For if Juliet and I become formally betrothed, Garrick would never do anything to humiliate me. Surely you can see that?"

Yes, certainly she could. Chivalry, thy name is Garrick. Or whatever.

"But what I fail to understand is why we're discussing the matter. Any reasonable woman would take any road to keep from marrying your odious Mr. Cox."

Well, he'd get no argument on that point, either.

"The thing is, Eliza, I'm sure to be missed at my own coming-of-age ball. And my father's already remarked on the fact that you left. They'll soon put two and two together and come haring down here. So either go get whatever you'll need for the journey or, so help me, I'll drag you out to my rig just as you are."

"But, Jervis," she began once more when he impatiently interrupted.

"Look, you can put all those arguments to me while we're driving. And I promise you, this is no abduction. If you don't come to agree that marrying me is the sensible thing to do, well, I swear it, I'll turn right around and bring you back. But at least let it be our own decision. Let's not allow our lives to be arranged by those people up there." He gestured dramatically in the direction of the Hall.

She knew she'd lost all grip upon her judgment when Jervis Wenham appeared to be making sense. But then, so be it. "I'll just take a minute," she suddenly decided, and sprinted up the stairs.

A quick survey of her portmanteau convinced her that it contained everything she'd need for an elopement and that her box could be left behind. She rolled up the traveling costume she'd planned to wear on her trip home the next day and stuffed it and a pair of slippers on the top. Then, with her bonnet in one hand and the portmanteau in the other, she tiptoed from the room.

As she and Jervis hurried down the graveled walk toward his waiting rig, Eliza had an eerie feeling that they were being watched. But if Betty was awake and had spied them, she made no move to interfere. Jervis handed her into the curricle, stored her bag away, and then jumped up beside her. He sprang his horses and they were off.

"Where is Gretna Green anyhow?" she inquired politely after they'd left the village well behind them and there was no sign of pursuit on the moon-lit road.

"Scotland."

"I thought so. Surely we don't have to go so far?"

"We do unless you happen to have a special license in your pocket."

"No need to be sarcastic."

The woods seemed eerily silent on either side, all the usual nocturnal noises of prowling creatures and singing insects temporarily stilled as they galloped by. Then off in the distance an owl hooted. One nearer the highway answered back. Eliza shivered.

"Scared?"

"Apprehensive."

"No need to be. We've a good head start, I collect. Not that anyone's necessarily going to try to stop us."

"They won't have to. If you keep up this pace, the horses will drop dead in their tracks."

"Don't try to tell me how to drive," he growled.

"Even Garrick says I'm a first-rate whip." None-theless, Jervis did slow down.

"You said we'd talk."

"All right then, talk."

"This whole thing is insane and you know it. We can't get married. We simply would not suit."

"We've been through all this before," he replied impatiently, "and I know we would. Oh, we may not be Romeo and Juliet—dammit, that's a curst example. Who's some other besotted couple?"

"*Garrick* and Juliet?"

"Well, yes, as a matter of fact." He glared.

"Well, I for one will have to have a better reason for matrimony than simply clearing the way for those two to wed."

"Really?" he mocked. "Well, then, how about Mr. Cox?"

"Oh, I'll admit he's a real incentive to elopement. And that's partly why I'm here. But it won't do. I'll simply have to stand up to him and Papa. Just as you and Lady Juliet need to stand up to your parents until you get this mess all sorted out."

"There's no way it's going to be sorted out. Even with his name cleared, Garrick's not half the catch that I am, and Juliet's parents are the ambitious types. That's why we have to elope, don't you see. For Lord Greenwood's bound to snap up Garrick's offer rather than have it appear that his daughter's been jilted by me. And now that his name's cleared, he's not really such a bad catch on the whole, even if he'll never be a viscount. Papa plans to turn the freehold estate over to him right away. I guess you'd call it compensation for the damage our family's done him. And Dr. Slaughter left him a competence. So Juliet won't be doing all that badly."

No, not all that badly. Eliza felt the prickle of tears and fought against them.

They lapsed into silence once more while Eliza renewed her struggle with her conscience. Heaven knew that she was tempted to go through with the elopement. With Garrick blissfully wed to his true love—why did she insist upon thinking in such flowery terms where those two were concerned? With Garrick and Lady Juliet *married*, why shouldn't she marry Jervis? She might be, as his grandmother had frequently pointed out, rather beneath his touch, but she'd certainly not put him to the blush. Hers was a proud, old family. Her father had earned a knighthood, after all.

Eliza's eyelids were growing heavy. It had been a long, trying evening. She gave them leave to close in order to make it easier to fantasize about being a viscountess, the mistress of Warleigh Hall.

She was blissfully building air castles in Cinderellaland when a vision of the wicked stepmother suddenly intruded. No, *two* wicked stepmothers, come to think on it. That really was the outside of enough. Marry Jervis and be in the same household with the ladies Wenham and Cheselden? No, it simply would not do! Still, she argued with herself, there was always the dower house. And one could grow accustomed to anything. Eliza was fast losing her grip on consciousness, sliding farther and farther into sleep. She jerked her nodding head back up. But the rhythm of the horses' hooves proved much too soporific. Eliza quit fighting her fatigue and gave in to it.

When the curricle at last pulled to a stop, she came to with a jerk and looked about her in bewilderment. The fading moonlight revealed a courtyard and a large square stone building adorned with bowed windows on both its upper and lower stories. "Are we there already?" she inquired.

"No, you pea-goose." Jervis sounded amused. "This ain't Gretna Green. It's the Black Swan. We need to rest the horses. And get something to eat ourselves. Hey, you there!" he called to a sleepy ostler.

Eliza stumbled across the inn yard beside him, trying to force herself awake. It was high time to do so, she chided herself, for dawn was now beginning to break. If she could only fool her body into thinking it had slept the night, she should then be in fine fettle.

Inside, she was aware of the curious glances from a handful of early risers, but she was far too tired to care. It wasn't until they'd settled themselves at a small, round table in a private parlor and she was pouring out cupfuls from a steaming pot of tea that part of the reason for the stares occurred to her. "Oh, good heavens! Our evening clothes. No wonder we look peculiar."

"We can change here. Another reason to stop."

Just then a waiter entered with a heavily laden tray and began to distribute its contents about the table. There was cold ham and beef, boiled eggs, plum cake, pound cake, light wigs, quodeny of pippins, orange marmalade, and chocolate as well as the tea. She would not have dreamed the country inn could provide so much bounty at such an early hour. Eliza helped herself liberally while Jervis did the same. He was looking pale and drawn, she noticed. The events of the night were beginning to take their toll. She hoped he was not in pain.

"Shouldn't we bespeak rooms here and rest a bit before going on?"

She had almost said "before turning back," for she'd made up her mind to do so, though just how or when the mental process had taken place she couldn't say. Perhaps it was while she'd slept that she'd decided it was unfair to take advantage of Jervis's temporarily distraught state of mind. He was convinced just now that he'd never love again. But he was young. He would recover. She'd simply have to persuade him to get out from under his mother's thumb. He could go to London for a season, attend Almack's. Perhaps he'd find another diamond of the first water at the exclusive social club, sparkling among next year's crop of matrimonial hopefuls.

"No, we mustn't stay here too long," he was saying. "We'll lose our head start. There's still a good chance of pursuit, you know."

And at that very moment, as if on cue, the parlor door swung open. Garrick Slaughter stood on the threshold, coolly surveying them.

"Good God!" Jervis yelped, springing to his feet and setting the dishes rattling. "What are *you* doing here? You're the last person I expected to come haring after us."

Before Mr. Slaughter could reply, Eliza gave her escort's sleeve an impatient tug. "Oh, do quit making a cake of yourself, Jervis, and ring for the waiter to bring more food. He's not chasing us, you pea-goose. He's also eloping. My, what a cozy group we make. Do stop your posturing, Mr. Slaughter, and ask Lady Juliet to come inside and join us."

Chapter
Twenty-one

Garrick ignored Eliza. His eyes were fastened on Jervis and there was a martial look in them that Savage Stenhouse would have recognized. He came striding across the room to grasp Jervis, who had gone even paler at the mention of Lady Juliet, by both his lapels. "It won't do, you know," he said softly between his teeth. "I've never begrudged you anything before, brat. Not your legitimacy, not the title, not our father's name. But this time, dammit, you've gone too far. You are not going to marry the woman I'm in love with. By God, I've a good notion to draw your cork." He released one lapel to draw back his fist threateningly.

"Stop it this instant!" Eliza jumped up to grab his arm. "Have you gone stark mad?"

"That's a deuced fine question," Jervis seconded. "I ain't afraid of you, Garrick, but dashed if I know what you're raving on about. I'm not marrying the woman you love. My God, didn't anybody tell you anything? What do you think this is all about? I took off before they could announce the betrothal. Eliza and I are going to Gretna Green to give you and Juliet a clear field."

"That's so," Eliza chimed in soothingly as she reseated herself at the table and took a liberal helping of cold beef. She had just discovered that she was starved. If this was to become her habitual reaction to high drama, she would soon pop out of her clothes. "Do sit down both of you and quit circling like snarling dogs. I take it then, Garrick, that you aren't eloping, but you thought that Jervis and Juliet were. Well, you're obviously mistaken, so do sit down and let's have our breakfast. Oh, by the by, when you came in breathing fire just now, who did you think I was, the chaperone? Or didn't you even bother to notice that Jervis was here with the wrong female?"

"What kind of an idiot do you take me for? Of course I knew perfectly well whom Jervis had eloped with. Why the devil do you think I ran my cattle to their knees to overtake the scurvy little dog-in-the-manger?"

"Oh, now, I say, really," Jervis protested as he obediently sat down and began to crack an egg-shell.

"And as for you"—Mr. Slaughter wheeled on Eliza—"you can damn well forget all your high-flown notions of being a viscountess."

"Oh, I already have," she replied rather thickly through a mouthful of beef. "No need to put yourself into a taking. I've no intention of marrying Jervis. Though why you should try to prevent it is beyond me. You were throwing me at his head earlier, if you recall."

"Oh, I recall all right," Garrick said bitterly, pulling out a chair and collapsing on it. "But that was before I realized I was in love with you."

Eliza choked. It took some vigorous back-slapping on Jervis's part before she recovered enough to gasp, "W-what did you say?"

"You heard me. I said I was in love with you."

"But—but you can't be!"

Jervis's face was at least as bewildered as Eliza's.

"Oh, can't I? I say, that food does look good. Jervis, ring for another plate." Garrick helped himself to a light wig. His eyes held Eliza's as he borrowed her knife to butter it. "No need to say 'can't' to me. I had no choice in the matter. I didn't know it, of course, but I suspect the damage was done when I first saw you being gulled by Gentleman Jack Oliver in the inn yard."

"Fustian!" She was on her feet again, glaring down at him. "You're head over heels in love with Lady Juliet, just as Jervis here is. And I don't mind saying that I'm sick and tired of being the pawn for both your noble renunciations. Well, I'm not having any more of it. Mr. Cox may be a loose fish, but he does want *me*."

"Oh, do sit down, Eliza." The waiter had appeared with a place setting and more provisions. Garrick watched him walk out the door, then remarked conversationally as he began to fill his plate, "Well, naturally I can't speak for Jervis, but *I'm* certainly not in love with Lady Juliet."

"You're not?" Jervis stared at his brother with disbelief. "Dammit, Garrick, Eliza's right. That is fustian. Everyone knows that you tumbled head over heels for Juliet at her come-out."

"Everyone knows that she was the most beautiful female I'd ever seen—sorry, Eliza, truth's truth. There was a whole group of us coves who were vying with one another for her attention. And"—he grinned impishly—"I won. She did stand up with me twice, you know, much to her mama's horror. But really, there wasn't much to it beyond that.

And in case you're both wondering, she's not in love with me, either. However, she *is* prostrated just now from being jilted by the man she does love. So I'd suggest you hare on back to the Hall, Jervis, and rectify the situation. Between here and there you should be able to concoct a plausible story to explain this hurly-burly."

"Are you sure?" Jervis had sprung to his feet, all the fatigue drained from his face, his eyes aglow.

"Of course I'm sure, stoopid. Go!"

Jervis hurried for the door, scarcely limping. He did have the grace to turn their way just after he'd opened it. "And you'll see to Eliza?" he asked sheepishly.

"From now on. Now leave us, halfling."

When the door had closed, the man and woman gazed at each other solemnly across the table. "It won't do, you know," she said quietly. "You've convinced him all right. But I know better. You see, I saw your face when Juliet and her mother were arriving at the Hall. You looked ... stricken. I've never seen such longing. Oh, you're in love with her all right."

He sighed and reached for her hand. She tried to pull it away, but he held on tightly. "Eliza, my darling, I've never denied that I *thought* I was in love with Juliet. My God, you've seen her. And please don't look like that. I'm trying to explain. I spied her across the ballroom floor and, dammit, she *was* a vision. And I'd had rather too much punch. By the by, have I mentioned that I've reformed my drinking habits, since so little good has come from them? Then there was the competition with those other coves to get her attention. I hesitate to admit this, but we'd even punted on it. After that, I did rather dangle after her during what I had left of the season. I think I was spurred on by the fact that her parents warned her away from me. That rather added to the challenge, don't you see. But none of it would have amounted to anything if I hadn't gone to prison. For let's face it, love, except for all that beauty, she's a bit . . . well, insipid. But during all those months in Newgate I had to cling to something, don't you see, or else go mad. So I'm rather afraid I turned Lady Juliet into a goddess. An object of worship, you might say."

"*You* might say." Eliza's sniff was eloquent.

"Anyhow, I do hope you aren't going to be jealous of her. I may have still been clinging to my fantasies when I first came out of prison, but I soon learned what it was like truly to be in love."

"Indeed?" Her voice was skeptical.

"Yes, indeed. No comparison. Once I'd gotten over my goddess obsession, I knew I'd never settle for anything less than a female of flesh and blood." He was sliding his chair closer.

"Oh, and just when was that?"

"I think," he replied seriously, "it was when you automatically believed in me. Juliet never did, you know. Please don't take that wrong. I'll admit it sounds quite self-centered. But, dammit, it's hard on a cove to be thought a thief. Plays the very devil with his self-respect. So your faith was a breath of fresh air, I must tell you."

"That's it, isn't it?" Eliza pushed him away as he tried to take her in his arms. "You were grateful. And when I managed to weasel a confession out of Lady Cheselden, then you really felt you owed me a debt of gratitude. Well, I can assure you—"

"Oh, the devil with explanations!" He pulled her roughly onto his lap and stopped her words effectively with his lips.

He had kissed her twice before, once under the handicap of a battered face, and she'd found both the experiences shattering. But they were but pale preludes to this lovemaking. Eliza emerged from the encounter feeling much as Savage Stenhouse must have felt as he lay stretched out from the knockout blow that Garrick had delivered.

He was looking at her searchingly and seemed well satisfied with her bemused condition. "Convinced? Well, I was always much better at action than at words. By the way, Miss Osborne, will you marry me?"

She nodded dumbly.

"Good. That's finally settled. We'll continue on then just as you'd planned, except with a change of bridegroom. And speaking of change, do you have anything to wear besides that tea-stained ball gown?"

Again she nodded.

"Eliza, my dearest, my own true love, while I grant you that now and again it might prove a rather pleasant change, I do hope you don't plan to remain mute throughout our married life." He frowned and waved his palm back and forth in front of her eyes. "Come on, sweetheart, snap out of it. You do understand that we're going to be married? In Gretna Green. Eliza?"

"Gretna Green?" Her voice was faint. "Gretna Green. Of course I remember Gretna Green. Isn't it in Scotland?"

FANCIFUL
FREEDOM OF FORM
EMPHASIZED THROUGH
IMAGINATION AND
EMOTION

Marian Devon